SPRING ON THE PENINSULA

SPRING ON THE PENINSULA

SPRING ON THE PENINSULA

A NOVEL

ERY SHIN

ASTRA HOUSE ⋀ NEW YORK

For information about permission to reproduce selections from this book,
please contact permissions@astrahouse.com.

This is a work of fiction. Names, characters, places, and incidents are
products of the author's imagination or are used fictitiously. Any resemblance
to actual events, locales, or persons, living or dead, is entirely coincidental.

Astra House
A Division of Astra Publishing House
astrahouse.com

Printed in the United States of America

Library of Congress Cataloging-in-Publication Data

Names: Shin, Ery, 1986- author.
Title: Spring on the peninsula : a novel / Ery Shin.
Description: First edition. | New York : Astra House, [2024] | Summary:
    "A sexually fluid narrator mourns a failed relationship over the course of
    two harsh winters in this raw, unprecedented portrait of millennials
    living in Seoul"— Provided by publisher.
Identifiers: LCCN 2023019502 | ISBN 9781662602221 (hardback) |
    ISBN 9781662602238 (ebook)
Subjects: LCGFT: Queer fiction. | Novels.
Classification: LCC PS3619.H574 S67 2023 | DDC 813/.6—dc23/eng/20230531
LC record available at https://lccn.loc.gov/2023019502

First edition
10 9 8 7 6 5 4 3 2 1

Design by Richard Oriolo
The text is set in Walbaum MT.
The titles are set in Displace.

부모님, 영관, 산드라, 그리고 윤정에게

SPRING ON THE PENINSULA

SPRING ON THE PENINSULA

THERE IS A street in Seoul where all the homosexuals go to buy drinks, linger, fall in love, or just spend the night in a love motel. (Or if they live alone, spend it where they live.) The last time Kai ventured there, it was quiet—a weekday, perhaps. He was not there to be coy but was there for food. Kai went there to eat street food under a plastic canopy with a few college friends of a child-hood friend, who were all now his good friends, affectionately esteemed. It had been a bitter spring, and everything and every-one seemed repulsive to him save for these faces. They spoke of love and the suffering it inflicts, the longing to return to the euphoria of childhood before such ordeals became common. These ordeals were rendered all the more tiresome by humiliations endured at the office, the insolence emanating from age-mates and superiors. Money was not a problem in this circle; love was.

Kai had recently been abandoned by a lover. The lover had left suddenly, simply vanishing one day. It was as though a parent had said goodbye to a child, and the child had left for school as usual but then never came home. Or a child went to school, and the parent never showed when pick-up time came. Or as though one lost one's sweetheart in a car accident, one's mother to cancer, one's father to alcoholism, then oneself to rape by a neighbor, followed by partial blindness after being hit by a bus, all in the span of a year (which happened to a friend Kai cherished, one of the unluckiest beings he knew). Or like an anecdote Kai's own father had told him about a classmate who had perished without warning overnight. Kai's father had recounted feeling the heat of that boy's arms around his chest—then, just like that, he was gone. Kai's father had told Kai about this, about Kai's father's younger self, about a peer he had known in middle school (or was it high school?) who had embraced him on their school soccer field. Everyone was laughing, having a good time, but the next day, the boy was reported dead because sometime in the middle of the night, his heart had given out. Hearing this story the first time had made Kai's own heart ache. The area over where Kai's heart was nestled contracted, palpitated. He remembered the sensation of moisture gathering around his eyes. Everything seemed so bittersweet and futile. Was life really like this? What an early bud destroyed. Smiling, laughing, husky embraces one moment morphing into nothingness the next. It had been exam season when Kai first heard this story. Such a sweet, aching feeling. Ah, grief!

The absence of Kai's lover invoked all these delicate sentiments at once. His absence made the forlorn Kai want to write everything down before the world was over, the private apocalypse came. At different times, the unholy magistrate comes for everyone. The species begins and ends in the same place, of course. So Kai pondered about carving out on paper a grand beginning and hopefully an adequate ending, and if things became sentimental somewhere in the middle, so sentimental they should be. There was nothing wrong with feeling sentiments; a taste for the melodramatic was even better! Moods had a way of being pleasant, changing here and there. They made life interesting, less staid. *Each day is the same, each day is different, but something needs to give at this point,* Kai thought. *At this stage in my life, I need something extra. It is too much of the same.* What he was experiencing was not a puerile, predictable boredom—just a little something inside that needed to be watered more frequently. Kai may have needed to get more air, let the north wind waft through, as they say. The story of what would happen to Kai was precisely that: of him treading around various surfaces at the same time he burrowed deep into that ripeness writers often speak about, that place in the heart of the ocean where one feels like one is collapsing under gravity's weight to become like those colorless fishes that exult in stillness, in the peace imposed by mountains of water. Kai's mother called this a very pure feeling. It is the peace of being thousands of fathoms deep during monsoon season. (It was, in fact, monsoon season on the peninsula when these thoughts were happening to Kai.)

Kai's friends asked about the end of the affair. *What happened? You devoted nearly a decade of your life to him. Why the long face, plumpy?* An elderly couple at a neighboring table was taking shots of soju while gossiping in a somber sort of way. The atmosphere at Kai's table was similar. The tone was raucous at first, but a melancholic air took over when he shared word of the failed affair. Kai became a pitiable creature in the group's eyes in that instant. But pride did not bar the orator from divulging yet more morsels of an intimacy gone sour. The mist enveloping the drinking tent on the sidewalk put Kai in the mood to wade deeper among the rushes. One cleared one's throat, yielded to that restlessness bundling up, hardening into caulk within. Ignored the slightly acrid smell coming from one's pits. Kai turned toward rapturous ears. *I wanted to go home. To be among the petals, the people I love. I thought we were the real thing. Yes, these platitudes bristle with truth. At age thirty-four, my lover had lost all ambition. No, he had never had any to begin with. His annual contracts were never renewed. There is nothing sorrier than a pretty but useless person. He was weak and insincere, betraying me by changing his mind at the last second about following me here. He thought he could, but he could not, he wrote. He lied to himself and me about having a future together. And then he changed his mind about changing his mind, leading me on for a year as I groveled by letter and phone. I begged him to reconsider even as I myself had begun to lose hope, pass into boredom. That last phase was memorable—a slow, billowing premonition, an unease that came down with such heft that I became flatulent most of the time.*

How Kai had internalized this loss was another matter. It circulated as all fine poisons do. It trembled and sputtered and congealed in Kai's viscera, turning his blood to brown lava. The stress of it all had given Kai angina and shingles—shingles! Cold sores can even form over one's nostrils, not solely on one's lips or inside one's mouth. A new day, a new lesson, but how disgusted Kai had become of such physiological revelations. How tedious. Unlike the face that still besieged his waking and slumbering hours, intruding upon those stray moments in between work and appointments with acquaintances who tried to entertain Kai or distract him from his ongoing humiliation.

The one who had absented himself from Kai's life had a thin, high-pitched voice. A relatively impoverished white-collar employee, Kai's former lover had not been self-assured. He clutched a number of insecurities—some valid, others not—regarding his education. He blamed others for his professional incompetence but was always the first to be let go from any workplace. An irritable hen, slightly autistic. Able to conflate both traditionally feminine and masculine qualities—an androgynous aura seductive to both sexes. Perceptive to Kai's tacit whims, especially in the act. When Kai rushed in to dominate, his ex-lover would comply by bouncing his rear up and down like a porn actress, moaning with relish, adding that touch of the theatrical Kai adored. He was the only one who understood to what extent Kai meant yes when Kai said no. Quite wonderfully impudent when bickering with strangers. A small egghead liable to making Michael Jackson noises, the *hee-hee*, when exuberant. Addicted to sharing online clips of his favorite songs, tugging at Kai's sleeve with the urgency of a spoiled child. Often came over to Kai's studio to take Kai out to lunch, but would end up napping on Kai's narrow spring bed. Stared at himself in windows when carrying beer crates across town. Good for making the house feel cozy when Kai had deadlines, bringing Kai food and fussing over Kai's half-buttoned cardigans as he grumbled to himself in a grandmotherly way. The silhouette of his back as he was lying down beside Kai, turned away—so sulky, so petulant. Wiggling his big toe, flaring his nostrils, proudly inhaling the mysterious stench gathering above his shoulders. The same shoulders begged to be butted in grocery stores. Shoving their cheekbones together, aligning his head with the stinker's, was one of Kai's favorite pastimes. Two or three hours past midnight, this person would draw near Kai and initiate sex while half-asleep. Such a complainer, being a light sleeper himself, about Kai's frequent trips during the night to urinate. Goats before the beheading ax could not have bleated more. He was impassive before aging and death, supremely impressing Kai. A man devoted to his extended family, comfortable with infants and senior citizens alike.

Above all, despite what was poor and paltry in him—the remnants of a vulgar upbringing—Kai's forsaker had been incredibly lovable. He was endearing in how he twisted his body kittenishly this way and that, prancing for Kai to lift Kai's spirits, prattling on and on about the mundane and the shocking according to Kai's moods, cooing, whimpering when he was hungry. He would pout in such a pretty way, scrunching his brows, puckering his lips and pushing them out, the lower lip fuller than the upper, both cold and wet rather than warm and dry. He was a darling at airports, waving goodbye sweetly, waddling a few meters forward, turning back, waving, calling out again, waddling forward and then glancing backward a few times more as a little duckling should. *What was it that he would say in the bath?* Kai scrunched his brow to remember. *We will be two dumplings that are rubbing paunches.* The darling would—and this was a memory Kai prayed would remain impervious to time and accumulated rage—emerge from the shower as he called out for Kai's attention. *Watch me, booby, watch me*, he would say, wanting Kai to watch his dancing. He called it the ding-a-ling dance, shaking his hips back and forth, delighted by his own stalk slapping from side to side, laughing and chortling like a cute little piglet all the while. What a piggy, so cute.

Kai no longer had any souvenirs from these days of happiness. There were no digital letters spared from mass deletion, no gifts left. Only some photographs and naughty videos had survived on a hard drive that Kai had hidden away in a desk drawer. No social media traces were available for reference either, Kai having erased all profiles in a bid to land a salaried position some years back. And no word from the departed ever since Kai had called him a silly faggot over email. Smarting under the knowledge that the deserter was almost certainly cavorting with others at present, Kai gave in to a rich despair whenever alone. What had made wiping the slate difficult was the way that he had kept contacting Kai after certain intervals, requesting the potential for reconciliation. These overtures tormented Kai with false hope. When he calmed down from whatever fresh bout had occurred, Kai went back to musing about how easily loyalties are subdued. It was as his parents said: couples who go their entire lives together wake up one morning, and it is over. Things seem invincible when one is in the thick of them, but their ends usually erupt out of nowhere. Love is prone to noble beginnings, anticlimactic finishes.

At least Kai's astonishment over his own shingles diagnosis lent him a modest amount of pleasure. It was a feat to contract shingles from heartbreak. Kai had never experienced such disquiet, not since he had dreamt of digging his brother out of the ground, his brother who had been buried headfirst in limestone. (The year Kai had been caught plagiarizing in high school was a close second.) What was the use of dwelling, however? Kai had had many lovers before this one, had been fêted for a roving eye and rakish charm. He had earned the right to be aloof at will. In the custom of the celebrated, then, it was better to cease fire lest he risk boring his audience. Everyone had their own problems. And Kai's settled friends could be insincere enough to claim that solitude was no burden when we remember how we go in and out of this world alone. Easy for them to say when they were not companionless. *They tell me I am being excessive in my grief,* Kai mused, *that I need not worry, I am succulent enough to ride it out, but I wonder if it works that way. I have little confidence I can start life over again like that. I am so tired, so very tired—I think this was it, this was the big one.* Kai regretted that he could no longer beat the one who left as badly as he had during their last fight. It had been a snowless winter. Kai had dislocated the insolent daisy's shoulder by pinning him to a wall, guffawing that if he did it again (Kai forgot what it was), the situation between them would grow very funny. Something luminous would get crumpled up quick, go dim in the slaughter.

But the table, the table. *Vanity and contempt will save you,* everyone murmured back. *Vanity for yourself, contempt for his lack of distinction, those petty fears trailing in his wake.* They were careful not to let pity or indifference inflect their voices. *You will not let yourself go, you will remain a catch. With him, you would have been the heir to two penniless households. Do not be anxious. There is a priceless desert of salt somewhere out there.*

What about you, what about you? Kai had become weary, was eager to change the subject. The friends looked at one another. Han was a naturopathic healer, Jung was a telecom consultant, and Min was a loafer. All were in their early thirties, with mediocre looks. Hardly mediocre, though, were Jung's exploits: the IT worker was the most ardent and inventive in bed. Kai could be interested in Jung.

Han and Min did not appeal to Kai in the same way. They were attractive in other ways. Kai did not bother drinking and carousing with people who were not personally likable. Han was tall and a bit of a literary dabbler. He had been tinkering with a story about a patriarch (a veiled stand-in for any of North Korea's autocrats) who coerces his starving people to feed on their own scabs; star-crossed lovers furiously dig a drainage pipe with their bare hands all the while. Min was not as tall as Han was, but still on the tall side. Their mutual friend, Yoon (absent tonight), was someone Kai liked most in the world. He was that friend from childhood who had gone to college with Min, Han, and Jung. Kai wanted to be friends with Yoon till the end.

Everyone wanted to stay friends with Yoon and to share their own anecdotes about him—now more than ever since he was going through a divorce, and there was much to talk about. He was a markedly glamorous figure for the four others, inspiring no little admiration bordering upon resentment for his aristocratic background and schooling, gentle personality, and exciting philandering life. Yoon was an only son born into genteel poverty. His mother's side of the family descended from royalty, but their wealth dried up once the noble clans had scattered at the dawn of the first republic. (His mother had been a salarywoman who died of sunstroke before her son had completed elementary school.) The new republic after the occupation had not been clever enough to exploit its nobility as figureheads for tourism and public relations as the English did, chasing them out with a rancor aggravated by self-doubt. By both temperament and circumstance, Yoon was inclined to drink more deeply of the world around him and his place in it. His thoughtfulness impressed Kai very much, not to mention his generosity of spirit, his unwillingness to indulge in fault-finding, his patience, his stoic demeanor, his softly affable way of talking, his way of refraining himself from touching his listeners whenever points of emphasis came up in conversation, his lack of body odor, and his habit of sighing when there was nothing to say.

Yoon had somehow managed to attend an expensive international secondary school that was established by Anglo-American missionaries around the turn of the twentieth century and catered to foreigners in the capital. That he had procured this privilege despite not being a foreigner himself was what unsettled his college acquaintances as well as Kai, thickening the bitterness that coated their weakness for him. Everyone present had all gone to local public schools.

Yoon's school nowadays resembled a private garden where non-Koreans and a steadily decreasing number of Korean Americans could thrive without becoming too familiar with the less well-off locals who watched from afar. During its earliest days, it had hosted a few Asian pupils: those who qualified as foreigners through their citizenship and cultural affiliations but were still too few in number to pose a serious challenge to the school's Caucasian core. As global travel and papers became more widely accessible across the decades, however, the school's trustees feared that their race ratio was tipping in an untoward direction. So the facility had grown whiter and whiter again in recent years, as the administration discreetly pushed to weed out the influx of nouveau riche locals who were born but not raised elsewhere. These Koreans were not the right Koreans. For these Koreans of the wrong kind, being born abroad was part of a ploy to gain foreign citizenship so as to gain admittance to the best secondary schools in Seoul, avoid military service (if they were male), and win a healthy discount in college tuition fees if they wished to study in the country of their citizenship.

The affluent Korean students whom the foreign administrators at Yoon's school did not like almost always had a clumsy grasp of

English and were culturally completely native, ignorant of American or European pop cultural references, humor, and less-than-mainstream music. They traveled to vacation resorts but were not well traveled in the cosmopolitan sense, chewing noisily with their mouths half-open during mealtimes, aided by a single utensil. None thought to use a fork and knife in separate hands at the same time. It was either a fork or chopsticks in the right hand until someone needed to cut something into pieces. Only then would they involve a knife, slicing everything in one go before putting that knife away and spearing the rest with a fork for the remainder of their meal. This style of consumption was their one coincidental Americanism that any good Western European would have shuddered before.

Han had many opinions about all of this. These kinds of cultural dynamics across history were one of his favorite drinking subjects. He was heating up to the night, eating, leaning forward, and smiling as he, in his own way, let Yoon have it: *Whether any Korean families, even those whose children fit the glumly third-cultural bill, earn an international school faculty's respect deep down remains uncertain. It is not exclusively a matter of their holding in contempt those who ignore a certain code of civilized behavior. It also has something to do with who these teacher types are. Yoon's old teachers were mostly religious-minded Midwesterners and South-erners from humble backgrounds. They moved here to rise to heights they could never have fathomed back home, giving themselves such airs before both our parvenus and their blue-blooded counterparts (who are still considered parvenus by Euro-American standards). The few teachers less insecure about their provincial origins may have been normal. None, minus a handful, ever learn Korean. This*

language barrier belies their community's alleged desire to assimilate.
Why go through the trouble of learning a tongue that lacks, say,
French's cultural prestige when locals will accommodate newcomers
in English anyway, ingratiating themselves in a fashion unthinkable
in wealthier nations with longer histories of winning wars and
technologically subduing the earth? Only the French, perhaps, could
intimidate this expatriate breed into taking language lessons. The
French, after all, make such a good show of showing off how inept
their English is. The French, unlike us, are too good for English.

France, Han liked to agitate when he got more briskly going
(usually around the time someone mentioned the Chinese, whom
he heroically despised), would not have Korea's lax attitude toward
civic order, with French laws of etiquette and human decency
forbidding the cutting of lines, the cutting of corners, all this grunting
and shoving to seize however much of whatever it was ahead of
the rest. For Han, the nation was an amalgamation of crude self-
interest (Machiavelli's caricatured vision to attain the ends at any
cost, minus his Italian refinement and sense of leisure), wide-scale
governmental corruption, and a materialism in which the gauche
rushed to compare luxury goods before Westerners who were abandoning such displays in favor of a Lutheran austerity. Anyone who
could speak English on the peninsula screamed it at the top of
their lungs, whether badly or adeptly, as a sign of status. *Look*,
they said, *I was monied enough to learn it. How elite I am!* (But
feeling mighty from being wealthy is a timeless, culturally universal feeling. Humans would rather choose status over objective
material and emotionally qualitative gains won through concerted
political action. They will sacrifice much for that affected feeling
of superiority, the pleasure of enforcing an inferior position upon

others.) The underground war between Korea's conservative factions who were in bed with America and its liberals who continued courting North Korea was endlessly boring since the metrics of what was considered truly liberal or libertarian in Seoul kept changing. It was unclear whether this bungling conservative figurehead was preferable over some other new blood in the same party when both kept pandering to young men who were frustrated by the nation's prohibitively high mortgage rates and their own vulnerability to accusations of sexual harassment.

A nation such as the Netherlands would never censor pornography over the internet, cigarettes on cable channels, or antipresidential criticism on the radio. Dutch drug policies would never allow citizens to be arrested back home for smoking marijuana abroad on the principle that the nation remains a fiefdom, with absolute ownership over anyone's actions across its borders. We might as well be living in North Korea or Singapore. Why is prostitution criminalized when there are tearooms, caffeineless coffee shops, and salons on every corner? If women are worried about sex trafficking and the concomitant rise of an even more outlandishly chauvinistic culture, we can set up male escort services by the thousands for harried professional women to even the playing field. Why do churches keep cropping up next to cabarets, ruining our fun? (Then again, how seriously Koreans take their religion is a point of debate in a land where love motels are reopened as churches in nightlife districts. To cut costs, congregations may decide to retain the electric billboards from the original buildings.) *Why do Catholics have a toehold here? It is bad enough dealing with yellow Protestants, let alone yellow Catholics and Mormons. With its tormented national past, Germany would never allow itself to be so complacent as to build a narrative where a president is ousted for letting a boat filled with adolescents sink. To hell with all this age segregation! Confucius should have been shot in a field somewhere. Why do people keep talking about those comfort women, attempting to wrangle more reparation money from the Japanese? We should worry about ourselves, our men raping our women like they did in that factory riot of the eighties when female workers protested in the nude for better conditions. How about we clean house first, mete out justice to those politicians guilty of sexual harassment, those male judges predisposed to being lenient toward male petitioners and the entertainment industry that operates like a soft rape ring? Look how many were ravaged by the Korean Army in Vietnam and the Philippines. Or how about the saddest story of all: seven pensioners who gang-raped a mentally impaired woman out of curiosity when she was a minor, and then again when she was an adult in her twenties? Why are you going home when everything is open late? Can anyone stomach the embarrassment over these native mothers running to the American embassy when their seafaring sons were sunk by Northern submarines? Just the other night, I heard one of them complaining about certain GIs tippling around the salon districts. Either tell Yankees to go home or hush if you need them the next day for housecleaning. True, they were imperious toward us after the Japanese left, but they are useful as heavies in a bovine way. While they are fanatically patriotic by Western European standards, at least Americans do not intrude upon the privacy of your home with personal announcements that remind you to hang out the national flag for Liberation Day. A voice does not drone from the ceiling, making requests that do not sound like requests. Why are these cosmetically altered minnows shouldering their way into an already bursting elevator? Doors are never held open. Why do black boxes have to be installed in every car as a defense against hyenas who are looking to make easy cash by throwing themselves in front of innocent cars or doing the old hit-and-run? Why do people keep buying cars that spontaneously combust? No wonder German companies laugh off Korean consumer complaints. The elderly will not refrain from coughing up their phlegm or swallowing it placidly in public. Everyone spits everywhere. Coffee is overpriced and of low quality. How can the world take this country seriously if its inhabitants cannot resist lying, cheating, gaming whatever system there is, buying beauty by going under the knife, and emulating Western trends in the most fulsome manner? How are we docile enough to let a patronizing Englishwoman take all the credit for poorly translating a prize-winning text? Everyone everywhere needs to reflect more subtly upon the philosophical implications of our era's realist-empirical ethos. The West fortunately spread a secular disdain for superstition and those ancient distinctions between men and women, the indigent and affluent, light and dark—and, irony of ironies, it advances, too, the word to recuperate one's ancestral heritage even as it is responsible for having eroded it from within for centuries. Too many invasions, too many marauders have exhausted the Korean sensibility. We have been cursed by generations of incompetent leaders. The Korean national character has sunk to its all-time low, now encouraging a prying instinct into the affairs, particularly minute shifts upward or downward in fortune, of one's neighbors and acquaintances. Korean popular music has become an international phenomenon despite originating in the drive to replicate Western music for Korean audiences. Koreans in the entertainment industry are plagiarizing sounds from around the world, particularly American hip-hop and*

European electronica, and ingeniously placing their own spin on things to sell them back to their source markets. Better yet, they hire foreign producers to make the same products, save with Korean lyrics. Songs and dances are presented as new things when they are the same old thing hidden behind slightly different faces. This is a roundabout trick to sell to the customer what they had originally traded in. Remember what that local choreographer did. He warned new studio arrivals that Korea had no choice but to follow American trends, smoking and pacing all the while before walking back into his office to rewatch hours of American dance footage, the work of mostly black choreographers hired by the industry's best. He watched such footage to copy those routines count by count, knowing there would be no legal repercussions, because how would copyright-holders see these routines in this new transpacific setting? Maybe some would, one could answer, since such plagiarism has become more difficult all around because now everything is documented online, but still the chances are small. Accusations rarely arise because of the tacitly patronizing but not wholly incorrect assumption that this is just what Koreans do, and what can one do but hold them to lower standards instead of the standards applied within network? If the West is now piqued by the East's music, but that music is but a veiled copy of its own, does that mean the West is very narcissistic? What blandness characterizes Korean cultural exports! Who can shake off that memory of those backup dancers and choreographers laying hands on one another's forearms, wheezing, We have no choice but to follow America?

When Han finally had a chance to pause and take a sip of beer, he would bring back the smiles with a pale quip or two. Something along the lines of: *At least none of us romanticize ourselves in the unbearable way that New Yorkers or Parisians do—that endless, narcissistic comparing between the old world and the new that only entrances those parties involved. We do not play with our food before we eat it as the cruel bullfighters do. We remain a cleanly race committed to public bathing. Give thanks this is not Rome in ruins (i.e., England). This is Seoul. And its skies look like clouds of semen dissolving in a muddy pond, its pollution keeping pace with its avarice. None are free yet here, but soon everyone will be once the peninsula recedes into the sea.* Yes, talking politics with Han was exciting.

All this is to say that admission to Yoon's school had been almost impossible back in his day. Even scions of the wealthiest Korean conglomerates were routinely denied entry. (So how, once more, had Yoon done it?) This rigorous form of quality control hinted at both the Western missionary's vanity and conscientiousness. The missionary rightfully takes pride in holding firm to principles in a land of the undisciplined. Today, one could not get by just with being a native English speaker (or a speaker of some European language with passable English on hand) and sporting a foreign passport. Both parents had to have international passports too. Those who survived the culling were an ideal mixture of well-to-do white Europeans; white Americans; white Latin Americans; a small subset of miscellaneous East and Southeast Asians as well as Middle Easterners; and Korean Americans whose parents were heads of state, industry, and combat. They were diplomats; politicians; civil servants; financiers; oil, technology, airline, or automobile magnates; intellectuals; or some other breed of white-collar professional.

The remainder of the offspring belonged to missionaries, the occasional shopkeeper, and lower military personnel whose ranks supplied the rare black child, the majority of black students being educated on military bases, not civilian centers. The children were polite and mild-mannered in general. Virtually no bullying occurred, as expulsions were only too happily meted out. Grade inflation was unheard of since parents were daunted by the presence of others waiting in the wings to assume their child's seat if they became too demanding or resentful of the school's imperialist power dynamics. Besides, the college admissions counselor was apathetic toward outcomes. It did not matter where any child went. Market demand would remain unruffled.

Yoon, were he out with everyone that evening, would have been pleased to point out that whatever theoretical inconsistencies arose between his school's founding mission and the exorbitant prices it charged for each student were resolved by way of practicalities. If families desired fewer missionaries in the classroom, ambitious funding was essential for courting better teaching talent. If parents could afford a chauffeur, that chauffeur required a parking spot as he waited for his ward at the end of the school day. As he was waiting and smoking, the children needed their fields of synthetic turf for athletic games and training, their revolving auditorium stages for artistic self-expression, their computer labs. Yoon never used a mocking tone when he spoke of these things. He was utterly, incandescently serious. He meant what he said because he had experienced the fruits of these gifts. Having them was better than not having them. They had made a difference in his life.

Had Han heard Yoon expounding on his educational stance like this, he would have fallen back upon one of his favorite pastimes: teasing Yoon about issues he went to great lengths to avoid. While he could not break through the barriers to entry at Yoon's school, Han had gamed his way through the national army, pocketing a cushy desk job like Yoon had through bribes. One of Han's hobbies was embarrassing Yoon about it. Han was probably ashamed of it as well, so rubbing Yoon's face in it was a superficial way to appear as though he himself was not bothered by it when he was. Both in their twenties had enjoyed being placed in non-combat roles as desk bureaucrats, while poorer men and a few women were assigned to submarines, regular warships, the infantry, aviation, and the like where someone could, in theory, be killed in combat. Yoon very much did not like to talk about this out of guilt while Han talked about it as much as he could for potentially the same reason, licking over this sore spot at every opportunity.

The friend group was eating and chatting and nodding among themselves about all this—and, again, love (including Yoon's lack of it for his soon-to-be former wife)—when someone walked by. He was very beautiful in a gentle, bean-like way. Spittle filled Kai's mouth. He adored munching on beans. Red, lima, soy, black, navy, kidney, garbanzo, pinto, cannellini, fava, tepary, mung, moth, velvet, peanut—good for every occasion, inexhaustible in nutrients. Red beans on shaved ice, brown beans mushed into a dipping sauce or a flavoring paste . . . Beans stoked Kai's craving for rice wine, not beer.

Begone, my sudden tears at the thought of someone else touching me. The tears that welled up in that flash surprised Kai. He had believed the gourd of grief was dry. *There is always something more*, he supposed, *beyond the gorge. Grief never stays where you think it is going to rest. You think it has spent itself, and it persists; you feel like luxuriating in it, but then only pickings are left to play with. Willful creature, this grief.*

Tangents would not do when Kai was endeavoring to pluck this bean from its pod. Kai readied for the opening bid. The table pleasurably tensed as a whole. Kai said, *Hey, you, you there!* The bean turned around: *Who, me?* Kai's friends nudged one another, being the semiprofessional titterers they were. Kai lazily eased out from under the tent and loped over to the man he had been eyeing. *My friends and I, we made a torture bet, you see. You are it for me; they dared me to bring you over, reel you in. Do you want to? If you come over, I win. We can have a few laughs together, drinks on us. Help me live this embarrassing moment down; it will be fun. My friends are veritable bastards but kind to strangers. Why not, how about it?* Kai pretended to be chagrined about rambling further, but no one had been rambling in earnest. Each word reverberated with purpose. Feigning to ramble is a higher art among the promiscuous. The act should endear the speaker to the listener, make the former seem artless, less practiced at fishing. Kai bunched his fist, beholding the hook sinking in just right. The bean hesitated a beat, then internally slackened, appeased by the crinkly, unaggressive, familial energy that Kai exuded as he led this master class in conversation. To be wholly emptied of want, detached from the goal of a certain evening, was the hardest part of crafting a situation where voluptuous instincts were to be coaxed out. *Ah, yes*, the bean bent, *All right, one drink to be nice. One drink cannot hurt.* Kai smirked on the inside. Hands clasped, mouthing, *Thank you*, he ushered the newcomer toward the table under what felt more and more like a tabernacle. Everyone settled in: *Hello, Hello there.* Without making eye contact with his trio of friends too directly, Jung most of all, Kai conveyed a warning: *Let us be careful not to speak in innuendos; no teasing him; be normal, friendly in a disinterested way.* Kai's company assented. So began the clucking over what the bean would like to drink and eat, a form of welcoming without overdoing the welcome. A delicate note must be struck in such meetings. Ugly, inexperienced people often bungle these things, veering them into tedium or unpleasantness. They do not know how to smile and lean in just enough.

None of this happened. It was too aggressive of a situation. No self-respecting pretty would accept such an invitation on the street, no one whom Kai would want to bed anyway. In real life, the bean floated by as the group snickered among themselves. *Kai, he is your type; you should go after him!* Everyone chuckled and felt merry and breezy by chirping in unison like this. The night was far from unpleasant. This was the way things should be. The friends crowed licentiously about how each would give it to the crunchity-crunch of a bean. In time, the conversation launched into the weightier matter of what a real encounter would require. It would mean meandering to a different location with a different atmosphere. Street drinking was, paradoxically, too emotionally cloistered. Tables were separated, the floor space yielding to obstructive arrangements of dining benches. None dared make conversation with other tables or request combining them together. The outdoor stall's very affordability as well as its public nature, combined with the industriousness of its typically middle-aged female owner, made it an ideal retreat for the working class and the working rich alike to air their sensitive grievances. It was where people of all ages milled around after the workday to refresh themselves. It was for families, lovers, friends, not for quarry. In search of dalliances, then, the group decided to get up. Han squared the bill.

On cue, everyone traipsed to a bar a few doors down that same street. The group wanted Kai to move on, and he could not do so on a sidewalk with eyeless night lamps peering down. *Yes, let us go hunting, yes.*

II

THE BAR THEY moved to next reminded Kai of a whale's belly: flesh-colored and cavernous. One opened a door, went up a fire escape, opened another door, and there it was. The tavern had two floors composed of recycled wood, a bevy of distressed pre-owned rugs from Turkey strewn everywhere, and soft red lighting reminiscent of that pervading wayside motels or slaughterhouses or butcheries after their alarms have been set upon closing time. Bathhouses emit a similar glow after hours, when no one is inside and their emptiness has been scrubbed emptier, the pools no longer rippling with bodies.

The group was winding its way into the whaling establishment. They were excited because this bar was something of a local legend. Only those who already knew where it was were there. There were no signs outside. The main entrance appeared no different from a portal leading into a personal domicile. A noir version of the Tangiers, a den without any opium, one powered by wordless, ethereal electronica, greeted the search party. To Kai's relief, there was no incense in the air. In his state, he felt as though he were floating in an aquarium. He felt as though he were paddling above figures huddled together on an ocean floor, entwined or sitting upright, mouths gaping open and shut in tandem.

The bass slowed. Someone, a shadowy pocket of a figure, approached Kai, flattering his vanity. Kai nodded, made grateful noises, but gestured at his friends, whose backs were receding down the stairs. Kai resumed walking, walking in a straight, straight line, following those backs till they halted in front of some cushions. Drinks came. Jung was sitting close to Kai, their knees touching with every shift in weight. *Maybe*, Kai thought.

When he drifted back into focus, Jung was telling a story about how a strange man had cursed at her when she herself had not planned on provoking anything. She had been on the highway. A driver behind her had begun tailing her too closely, eventually yelling profanities at her and then speeding past. When she found herself at the same rest station with the curser half an hour later, Jung was furious but content to stare him down. She had not wanted to go further than this. To get in his face, spew curses back, or become physical stoked fear in her heart. The man may not have been normal, liable to maul her for muttering to the side—what then?

In her dreams months later, months after the fact, her astral twin would have no such qualms. She would track the curser down by a fountain outside the men's room, informing him not to yell at women in cars, asking him why he had done such a thing when she was respecting the speed limit, assuaging his masculine pride by asking if there was something wrong that day, a happening he had to attend to; could she help? She would win a sheepish apology from this attacker who had emasculated the virile being she was. But her passiveness in actuality during that decisive moment had made Jung feel cowardly, like she had been careful for nothing. Jung's mother had warned her not to push things with strangers. One never knew what could happen. It was better to be safe than sorry. A man could hurt a woman if riled up properly.

Jung had not elevated herself beyond such consequences. She was low enough to worry about them.

At work, Jung resented a certain manager on her floor. He would make such a display of serving himself last at office lunches since leaders eat last, at least according to a book he had read after his wife had given birth to their second child. He wanted his expanded fatherhood to mean something. He wanted the occasion of his youngest's birth to commemorate something nobler in himself. But his lunch show was all a part, Jung was convinced, of a broader intellectual vanity that people indulged when they felt just as immature after undergoing a rite that was supposed to have matured them and so wanted to overcompensate for this uneasy feeling.

This fable of family-making that new mothers and fathers enshrined bored Jung. Having children makes people feel better. Parenthood makes people feel the cozy guarantee of eventual elder care despite the fact that their children remain as equally neglectful to them as they were to their own parents a generation ago. Children of any age, grown-ups included, are selfish and callous to their parents, so why would they want to breed their own? Only those who were good children should have children, but such logic would leave the world with not that many people. The fiction of the family is—and how many authors have repeated this?—just fiction.

Jung would later go on to have children with someone she had not anticipated, and she would come to understand that children are not merely lifestyle choices. Years before this happened, however, she had felt differently. The above is what she had felt. Only later would she realize that she had been more circumspect than most about family planning out of her own guilt from having been an aggressively unpleasant child to her parents. She had attributed an emotional drabness to them that was not theirs when they were often more progressive in spirit than she herself was. Unlike her daughter, for instance, Jung's mother believed that by learning to be content with everyone's circumstances, a person could successfully associate with someone who made a more modest living. There was no need to avoid modest earners entirely in the marriage market.

Jung's father was not one to fall behind his wife in such personal liberalisms. He had once told his daughter that if she chose to go with a blue-collar worker, that was a choice that only she could make for herself. No one from the family would intervene. He would respect her wishes. *Parents cannot win over their children in such matters*, Jung's father would assert while shaking his head. It would be years until Jung learned to give both of her parents enough recognition. The freedom that they had won in their own right was the right to be different, to be independent of their own parents by gradually refusing to take responsibility for them.

Jung's office manager reminded her of another unpleasant acquaintance encountered at a recent gathering. In this acquaintance's bid to raise herself in everyone's esteem at the time, she would not let the others speak ill about a mutual friend who wanted to be a doctor after having been a homemaker for close to a decade. This aspiring doctor had finally decided to attend medical school in her early thirties, motivating everyone in a room elsewhere to sigh with worry. Jung's acquaintance became too protective then, taking it upon herself to speak against everyone who had raised concerns regarding that friend's decision to start medical school. She said the aspiring doctor would be fine, but she said it too sharply, even ostentatiously. Her sentiments were admirable, but she was making too great a show of them, perceiving the collective's stray comments as condescending attacks when they were less than nothing, more like polite expressions of interest in another's life—certainly not statements to merit an aggression that made everyone feel uncomfortable and want to leave the event early.

This self-indulgent person had created tension on another night out in a different city. When Jung's circle had their fill and were ready to head back to the hotel room they had rented for the night, one among them spread the word that she was going home with a stranger. The others wished her luck, but Jung's unpleasant acquaintance made another show of herself by insisting that the lone bird bring her new friend back to their hotel. That way, the night could rest easy. This act may have seemed considerate, but its shrill undercurrent made it more about that acquaintance showing off what a good friend she was. Everyone else, by this line of thought, became an accessory.

This acquaintance of Jung's herself had a friend (with whom Jung was better acquainted) who had an unpleasant way of acting like a bird's beak, of beadily measuring the goods and transactions around her, verbally jabbing those in her vicinity if she grew resentful and her personal threshold turned over. Her habit of hawking about and calculating someone else's expenses and attributing them to sprees when they were not sprees but the result of ordinary shopping made Jung wary. More and more for Jung, this friend was an ambiguous presence, especially when this friend grew defensive about her own finances. She suspected that others judged her for a lack of thrift when no one was thinking ill of her. Her temperament made her behave in too forward a manner in certain situations, impelling her to ask with inappropriate specificity about the cost of things, peeking out from beneath her lashes when cash was being exchanged around the table. If someone opened their wallet to lend money to another, she would almost certainly catch them in that moment. No, she was not one to miss an exchange.

Neither was the waitress who had wounded Jung's father's feelings at a Korean-Chinese restaurant a few weeks past. The family of three that night (the fourth and fifth members were out on their own for the evening with co-workers) had ordered only one serving, but not because they did not have the right amount of money to cover the bill. No one was that hungry that night, and everyone was health-conscious and averse to the sensation of eating more than was necessary—and even more so if this act of dining was just for appearances before a restaurant's waiting staff. The family kept nibbling away and picking at their two dishes, one small appetizer and one main course, in a red satin-filled room. As Jung's family was leaving, one of the older waitresses looked at Jung's father without looking at his eyes directly and rasped, *Is that all you ate tonight, sir?*—the implication being that his tab was too miserly for his party's number, not enough to compensate the staff for their time and service. Three seats had been taken out and dusted, but why should they have been in these circumstances? Her accusing him of stinginess and underbreeding smote him in the heart, as he was a sensitive, educated man. To be accused of being unaware of dining norms was a great hurt for him, as he prided himself on his civility and for holding certain standards.

The faces and bodies that had aggravated Jung proliferated as she kept telling stories that were inspired by other stories inspired by the highway incident. These stories were not that short, yet they did not take up too much time, as Jung shared only a few before letting the conversation move on (the rest she recounted in her mind alone). But in her marrow, her seething did not cease. Each episode brought forth other memories of people who had irritated her, rubbing her as asphalt would.

Everyone is a burden on everyone who knows them as well as strangers. Jung no longer wanted to accommodate anyone, not even her family, regretting the degree to which she had hitherto indulged those around her. Those who were unpunctual for events they themselves organized, who thought their time was more important than others', who believed they deserved favors wherever they went—Jung more and more frequently found herself disliking her companions.

Or maybe she had never liked anyone, and this misanthropic impulse was what united her and Kai, forging the basis for their mutual attraction. Jung did not really enjoy people, particularly the female sex (which she had no issue identifying with while perceiving herself to be a woman apart). She felt women to be as yet incapable of irradiating that magnanimity borne of centuries of learned leisure and access to sexual frivolities. Women, the as-yet lower caste, carried themselves in too fastidious a fashion for Jung's liking. They constantly lied, moreover, about their inferiority, exulting in some superior feminine absolute when such overstatements only highlighted their impotence. If women were strong as a matter of course, why would anyone need to reiterate this? If a hole is full, it is redundant to keep underscoring the soil's weight that fills it. Only out of an ongoing lack comes this insistence on a woman's strength that is a reminder of her weakness and debasement. No, Jung did not like women.

As Jung waded deeper into her pet hatreds, one vague, uneasy memory billowed up of her father telling her that if she continued to be so ungenerous, there would be no one left around her. Who could withstand her fondness for cutting others down, uprooting them without planting a future? The tides would turn against her, the majority would return her animosities in kind, and there would be no conviction held by anyone about her, a person whose name was *Jung*, such a freighted word.

Kai kept drifting as Jung was laughing and grumbling about work and people and travel. He was worried that the rugs in this bar were too far apart. The same problem that had arisen in the street stand was happening all over again. The bar's layout made it hard for different groups to mingle. This was a real worry despite the nicely distracting sensation of Jung's knees grazing his own every so often. Kai could see it now: carving Jung up with Yoon watching or having Yoon in on it too if Yoon were feeling game. That would be a treat. Jung would like that a lot.

Almost without realizing it, Kai found himself moving toward the staff zone. There was an enclave to the side where bartenders and servers congregated. It was not a sitting area for customers, as there were no chairs laid out, but a serving area where outgoing drinks and nibbles for customers were made. Kai headed there because he wanted to move around, stop sitting so much. He wanted air and exercise. He could use some space from Jung, whose special company could be had at a later date. There was no point in honing in on a readily available menu item on a night such as this when entirely new and more exclusive restaurants could be visited. Besides, he was unprepared tonight; he did not want to unbutton Jung's shirt without a tripod in the room. He wanted to remember this one, would be unhappy if their night together were reduced merely to phone recordings. That kind of amateur hour would be nettling, was no good for Jung. Jung deserved the best from him. Kai's cheeks had been flushed for some time now. The alcohol's effects were dispersing throughout his body in a rapturous flush. He was loosening up, feeling better. The stranger he had shooed away earlier by the stairwell had been a nice forget-me-not to start the night off right. A year ago, Kai would have taken such attention for granted. It was cherished now.

Kai reached the drinks aisle and looked around. There was only one bartender present. The server for Kai's table had gone out for a cigarette break.

Yes?

Yes, we need more drinks, the same we ordered on the last round.

Kai looked at the bartender straight on for the first time. Kai smiled in an unaffected way, not breaking eye contact as he ordered some food on top of these drinks, some wet and dried squid marinated in this-that pepper paste—additional cutlery, small plates, and cups for an extra pitcher, too, come to think of it. The order was neither rushed nor rambling. It was amiable and to the point. The bartender said he understood and promised to bring everything out.

Kai returned to his table, which had turned raucous. His friends were in great spirits that night—chatty, careful not to disturb other tables, still sober enough. *Shall we play a game once what is new arrives?* The others were ignorant of Kai's newfound interest. He had not bothered to let them in on it. That would taint it. It was bad luck to share where the hunt was going before the quarry was in sight. There he was. The food and drinks arrived with the bartender, not Kai's original server. If they had arrived with the latter, now returned from his break in fine form, that would have been frustrating. But they had not—Kai's bartender-cum-server walked up with a tray balanced in both hands until he could kneel by the table. He was talkative in a sedate fashion. As he placed everything down and about, he asked whether they were regulars around the block. There was a searchingness there. He even became flattering, asking whether they were college students, peering mostly at Kai without moving his features too much. An expressive face could come later.

The group noticed. *That thick-lidded, sleepy-looking fellow might be interested in you*, they told Kai after the bartender had bowed and left. Kai shared a quick *Maybe, let us see.* Let us see indeed. The conversation kept going, but Kai's head was no longer in it. His mind was on that bartender. The water tasted good that night. It was time for games. The quartet took shots every time one of them stumbled over their arithmetic. Whenever someone flicked the wire hanging off a screw cap, down went the contents of a bottle. *Never have I ever. Have you? Yes.* Min drained a third of a pitcher containing beer mixed with soju, and Han grew more inspired. Jung's blouse was slipping lower as she kept leaning forward toward Kai. If she wanted Kai to see it, he was seeing it. Her limbs stayed supple when Kai placed his arm around her shoulder, caressing her cheeks and upper arms, alternately chiding and congratulating her for finishing her drinks. Kai's bartender came again to clear away empty glasses and dishes. He kept coming back to tidy up and refill things. Each time he came around, the remarks that passed between him and the table grew more familiar. The group affirmed how atmospheric the place was, how glad they were to have ended up there that night, and how it was hard but not so hard as to be too hard to find its entryway from the street. By the time the question of whether the bartender would join Kai's circle for a drink floated to the surface, as though buoyed by beer mats, it felt natural for him to say yes, rude to say no. He sat as he was asked to do without fanfare or forwardness.

He ended up sitting next to Kai. Jung kept her place by Kai's other side. She had given Kai a long, sly look when the bartender had gone to fetch something for the table before joining them. Kai had said, *Hey*, and patted her lower back a few times while laughing in response to that look. He could feel Jung was not jealous now. No, she was content to talk loudly at this table of her friends, found her delights in drinking competitively under his affable caresses, his glances. That she would say yes to him on another night half a year later was not clear to her yet, even if it was clear to Kai. She would, she did, but this night before that all happened, Kai felt that Jung was showing signs of wanting to air certain linens out without buying new ones. Jung must have suffered tremendously at work that week, as she was evincing an aura of burnout that had to be treated with much platonic consideration—like staying with her on a bench somewhere; letting her rest her head in his lap; draping his coat over her when she grew good and drunk, gone enough to drool with her mouth open, before dropping her off in a cab at the condo she shared with both of her parents;

holding her purse all throughout to make sure it stayed hers as she enjoyed the gale. Han would take care of her tonight, Kai knew. *When I do it, I will not send her home. She knows that and will linger then.*

When Kai and Jung actually ended up in that place later-later, Yoon was not a part of it. There was no recording camera. Jung took it fast and hard and noiselessly but needed time to properly climax in Kai's mouth. After both were done, Jung admitted it had felt abrupt at first but good over time. *Could Kai make her feel good again?* He did, over and over that night to the point of anemic collapse, so resolutely did he and Jung crawl together, clinging to each other as shackled beasts do without thought for the future.

Goodbye, Jung, for now. Hours later, the group had gone home. Kai remained behind at another bar with his bartender for about another hour until they got up. The two had decided to move to a love motel nearby, but the way in which Kai's newfound companion finessed this transition had been particularly graceful. Sensing Kai's openness, the bartender divulged a classically masculine temperament. He poured drinks and made light conversation, chuckled occasionally, offered his lighter at appropriate intervals, and was careful not to give the impression of being someone who was frivolous or undignified or humorless or miserly. He was genial without appearing unconfident. The two shared life stories about where each had lived, their jobs, their daily schedules, what Kai's friends were like when they were not at the bartender's bar, what other bars the group frequented, where they liked going out in Seoul, other parts of the world they had visited, where each wanted to visit, fitness regimes, recreational activities, music, movies, siblings. First loves, first times, and recent affairs were the last order of the day. These last confessions would whet their palate for what was coming next. The fuzzy feeling from alcohol was clearing away. Kai and the bartender both admitted with mirth to having lost their virginities at fourteen. For the bartender, this happened at someone's house when the adults were away on a night shift. It had been casual and unrushed. Everything was tight and a bit dry in the beginning, but saliva and tender fingerings had smoothened the rest of the act. The bartender and his first had remained friends afterward, until everyone went their own way for the draft.

Kai never saw his first after their one night together. His first was a herald for what was happening now. Two hours before sunrise, the bartender asked Kai about his intent. *The subways are closed now. Shall we rest somewhere in the meantime? It has been a long night for me too.*

That would be restful, yes, Kai affirmed, as if granting a concession. The room was tinted blue. *It is like that first time in that first room,* Kai thought to himself. There was the same big mirror mounted on the wall, a similar Renaissance painting stapled to the ceiling above the bed. A modest bathroom to the side could be glimpsed. They entered that bathroom together after they were through. The bartender expressed his annoyance when Kai, overcome by a wave of perverseness, would not let him get up and out of the small tub they had been sharing until that point. Every time he tried to move, Kai tensed his legs around his waist, holding the impasse. Kai could see the bartender thinking that his legs would start cramping soon unless he found a way out without making things awkward. Kai did not linger after the bartender finally made his escape to dry himself off by the bed, looking at Kai strangely. Their night together was not followed by ox bone soup the morning after like Kai's first time.

These bouts of meeting and going away continued into the fall and winter that year. In DVD rooms, karaoke rooms, PC rooms, arcades, tearooms, coffee rooms, salons, any kind of room that was faintly or intensely disreputable, Kai made nighttime friends and tried to gather handsome memories before work called everyone away. Such habits had a soothing effect on him.

Then something funny happened: Kai hit a wall, running into it as he turned the corner in an alley. Embarrassed, he hit the wall again, this time with an open palm, rebuking it: *Hey, you, that hurt! You bad thing, you!* As a small child, Kai had adored when his parents would pretend to beat objects that got in his way. When a building block tripped him or a table corner dented his forehead, that poor little piece of wood, plastic, brick, cement, or whatever it was would receive a thrashing from the grown-ups. The tone of voice they had wielded on those occasions was lovely in its authoritativeness. The wall that had leapt out at Kai brought back these feelings. It evoked such wistfulness for these two figures who had loomed over him during past times. Would they loom over Kai now? The wall motivated him to visit his mother and father in the countryside without delay. It was time to go home and refresh himself. Everyone Kai had been meeting had begun bleeding into one another, looking and behaving and smelling the same to him, with all their life stories assuming the same patterns of studied diffidence, banter, omissions, and so forth. No one was exceptional but a shaving of a type in a broader system of nondescription.

There was another reason Kai was eager to leave the city. A hairdresser whom Kai had been supporting was starting to stir up problems now that it was winter. If the bartender had been a hummingbird in an aviary, this woman was an albatross. She summoned flames neither hot nor cool in Kai. She was no one any of Kai's daytime friends would know, being a nondescript member of a type like the other types of people that Kai was contenting himself with: full-time students, professional moonlighters, semiprofessional athletes, struggling musicians, minor artists, vendors, caterers, copy editors (never writers), boiler repairers, friends out on leave from the army for a night, and nightlife staff. Grief was dulling Kai to the point where he needed stronger sensations to escape boredom.

This woman was not a salon hostess, or yet another unlucky actress, or some stooge branded by the underworld, or a plastic surgeon's assistant emaciating herself to keep up appearances, but a hairdresser Kai had met on a Friday when everyone else had left to enjoy the weekend. She had been responsible for closing that night. Kai usually did not speak when he needed his hair attended to, but this hairdresser was careful not to be nosy or enervating in her questions, which were evenly spaced apart, no more than a handful total as Kai dozed in his chair. She sounded out her words slowly through a throaty, yawning voice. Conspicuously attentive about reading Kai's lips, she kept touching her hair, rearranging it behind her ears. Kai noticed these things. He had only snapped to attention, however, when she asked him whether he had someone. *No, I am unattached. What about you?* Her shaking no, she had no one, settled the matter. Kai left with her contact information.

Their first time together had been gratifyingly forced for Kai. Kai had forced things along. She had acquiesced, revealing a docility that he found winning. After a movie, during which they held hands until body heat and clamminess discouraged them, and after dinner at a barbecue place, they decided to go to a DVD room. A motel was too soon for where they were. They had not even kissed yet. Kai asked her to choose the film. She chose something by a youthful Greek director, a hospital drama led by an actress with a breathy way of giving speeches. Kai leaned in. She was confused when he started kissing her shoulder, moving up along the side of her neck within two minutes of the film's opening. *It is too early for that*, Kai could see her thinking as she drew back from him, looking at him strangely. Her confusion would turn to startlement, then terror, then repulsion, hoarse shouting, and an early departure if Kai were not careful. It was too bad he had to be careful now instead of honest. If they had not been out in public, he would not have cared, but they were. So Kai took care to make his hands very gentle, stroking her face and hair in a slightly timid way, tongue-kissing her in between pauses and chaste kisses. His hands never ceased moving, caressing her into calmness, reinforcing her vanity, giving her a safe, luxurious feeling. Kissing her with an open mouth, a closed mouth, a deep tongue, light tongue flicks; stroking above her shoulders in a leisurely, soft way; saying nothing, no whispers or groans to disrupt her amorous feeling. A few minutes later, he could move his hands downward, then downward still. The woman was completely undressed now. She was being orally pleasured and fingered as she, under Kai's guidance, held her own buttocks apart, with Kai pushing his wet fingers down her throat every so often to excite her.

When they came to know each other better over the next few weeks, the hairdresser let Kai borrow one of her professional razors to shave off her genital hair over a toilet basin. Another day, she knelt on the ground with her back arched and her buttocks prettily pushed out, and kept her head and mouth where Kai wanted her to until he was ready, even though he could tell her jaws were locking and she was tired. She was efficient both at work and in Kai's presence, understanding what was wanted without having to be told. Her ankles held up high, feet dangling, legs slung over Kai's shoulder as he slapped into her, she was admirable for being a good sport when she was dry. Kai liked clamping her wrists down by her sides as she lay on her back, her bosom bouncing everywhere under his lively pounding—what a sight, her mouth set in a faint grimace, drooling. *Mew for me, Auntie, I cannot hear you.* The way she would sob for Kai was unearthly, a long, husky keen like what a whale would let out when it sinks to the ocean floor, a sound punctuated by rasping heaves when he ground into her as far as he could go. She became his most regular nighttime friend.

Kai could never tell whether she came or not, even though she said she usually did. He would hold his hand over her throat to check for vibrations. Did they signal the same thing every time? But Kai was decent in his own way. He made sure to give her as much pocket money as he could afford whenever they met. All their meals and date activities were taken care of by him. He never forced her to take the lead in bed or work very hard at it. He was the more active, industrious one; she mostly had the fun of being pleasured, being lazy. Kai never made her feel bad about her face or weight. He kept giving her money until he did not feel like it anymore.

When someone wants money from someone else to tide them over, it is never the way books say it is. It is a sad sight to see, a bad taste to taste. She would sit there like a lump, lingering over her drink until Kai lost his patience, asking her what she was waiting for. This woman was not a mistake, but it was time to let her be for a while, maybe indefinitely. It is depressing for people to feel that others are not their equals, beneath them in every way and grasping on top of everything else. It is gloomy if one side always submits to the other without any glimmer of unpredictability or egoism. Contempt bars the way to deeper communion. Poverty spiritually maims people. It makes dilapidated houses out of them. In the hairdresser's case, it forged an abyss where her stomach should have been. It made her too grateful and not grateful enough. Kai wanted to retch every time she would dart forward and snatch free items she did not need at hotels or department stores.

Is it any wonder that he prayed, *Begone, winter*? Working in a pastoral retreat would help distract him from this depressed feeling. Like a snake devouring its own tail while its torso lengthens, Kai would renew himself through work, beget himself again. Work would make him what his own mother and father were to him. Sometimes this talk of adult diversions—hairdressers, bartenders, all of it—invokes its own sense of monotony. Even animals relieve themselves in between rounds. Here and there, the living step back for a moment before they can reimmerse themselves in their sensuously immediate realities.

III

IN MANY WAYS, time is elusive and shifting. In others, it is terribly linear. Terrifyingly straightforward, devoid of any sense of humor. The distance between Kai's projected elderly self and his childhood self was closing. But it was closing faster for his parents, a phenomenon he could not accept. How long ago was it when Kai had placed his palm on the mirror as a child in the en suite bathroom of the bedroom belonging to his parents? The child had drunk in his own image, imagining at the same stroke an older face that would take the place of his own at present. Kai's parents were now at that older age. Like a city of stone soldiers surging forward, time had overtaken the couple. Kai was inconsolable. Was it cottonwood or snow falling? Would Kai be able to tell the difference when he likewise succumbed to time? Time would be more merciless then. Despite what philosophers like to tell themselves regarding what is right and able to be done—how time can be reconceptualized outside the linear framework—Kai could not partake in their timeless feeling. He knew better: time goes one way. Look for the parents of the parents of your parents, and you see. Who is there? There is no one. Weather is weather. Clouds move on.

Humans are never as mysterious as they hope to be. Having reached the end of his private coastline, Kai was on a train to Chungnam, the province of the Yellow Mountain, to pay his respects to his unretired parents. Kai loved them very much. They were close to him. Kai had no extended family, not since a fight over wills had erupted on all sides. Kai's parents had been left with nothing by their parents. Everything had gone to their siblings. Kai's mother and father moved on. They did not let their hurt fester.

Kai's mother was the type to not get upset over broken plates. She had patience for clumsiness. She would clean up after such accidents without berating anyone. Dishes that were wrongly fetched at restaurants or did not taste the way servers said they would were consumed without complaint. Kai's mother would say it was all right, a drink or dish was also delicious if it was a gift, something that serendipity had saved for her. She could be exacting, but that trait was evaporating. Time was mellowing her spirit.

Because her own father had been stringent at home, enforcing quietness upon his wife and children with a fanatic's ardor, Kai's mother chose to live with a man who visited other temples. Her husband, Kai's father, was the lenient, doting, whimsical sort, prone to making jokes about finding the right holes, about whether bigger things felt better than smaller ones to her. He never raised his voice at her, as he did not doubt that she was her father's daughter. Kai's father was a man without a past: there were no pictures taken of him in his childhood. He had to borrow yearbooks from his friends to see his school pictures. There had been no toys for him as a child, only books. In this way, he was like Kai's mother. He wept if anyone around him or on television wept bitterly. Such a dancer, better than his wife, although he was lazier than her (in small, never big, ways). He had spoiled Kai as a child by driving him everywhere in Seoul, to the point where his son had not known how to take public transportation until he entered late middle school. He possessed a diplomat's verve without its greasy aftertaste, letting Kai enjoy processed treats when his wife was not watching. Kai's father would rather be seen as gullible than too harsh on someone. He did not mind being lectured out in the open by his wife and Kai, although he could become morose as it was happening and after. He once threw a newspaper roll at Kai's head, neither that hard nor straight on since it fell to the side somewhere, but had felt so jolted by his own outburst—what he experienced as an alien brutality—that he came right away to Kai's room, where Kai was resting, to apologize with an embrace.

The father of Kai's mother had been a slender person who ate a lot of caramel and became diabetic, although it was uncertain whether this was because of the caramel or his genetic predisposition. He was respected by his eldest daughter, Kai's mother, but whether he was liked by her—that was uncertain. She loved her mother, respected her father, but did that respect include love? Since he had chosen to make a living by going into business at a young age, when circumstances were difficult in the Korean War's aftermath, he had always carried a large amount of regret about his lack of schooling. He had wanted to receive a formal education, but finances have a way of complicating a life. Money matters may mold it in another direction, not necessarily a bad one, only different, at times bitter-tasting for those who do not get a choice. It was too bad that his wife, whom Kai's mother had loved with the chivalric fervor of a vassal before their sovereign, had cut her daughter out of her inheritance.

It was a shame that that family loved its sons over its daughters. That in itself was not abnormal for older generations and even today's. This is the law on the peninsula, once explicit, now unspoken. Kai's mother would be glad when it finally changed, although it had not changed fully yet. Her brothers, who had been submissive to her before, grew emboldened after their patriarch's passing, doing their best to convince their mother to disinherit her most loyal shield. Kai's uncles wept a great deal at their father's deathbed, as if they were trying to water the hole in their father's cancerous throat.

Peace reigned over Kai's household because his mother and father both worked outside the home and were united in their interest in having a loving and modest homelife. Learning was important for both figures, as was being industrious and social in independent circles. Too many couples nowadays cannot do anything without being together. Kai's parents liked each other very much and were companionable, sometimes in a sickening way in front of Kai, who would grumble indulgently. They had locked their bedroom door at night when Kai was a child. Their door stayed locked on certain nights even during some of Kai's visits now.

If Kai's parents had any foibles, it was that they could not see where they were too possessive about their own children. They were not always as liberal as they wanted to be. They would never have accepted someone like Kai's hairdresser into their family. Whatever was done with people like that had to remain a secret that did not stir ripples above. One had to have standards. A love like that would be a sterile love, its ending already inseminated into its beginning.

While a childish part of Kai blamed his parents for his aloneness, for how the pedestal they had raised for him had room for only one, his greater love for them stemmed from their loving moderation. They were expressive, gentle-hearted people who could be reasoned with. They did not like extremes or hard answers. They did not take their goals and passions too seriously. They were happy cynics. They softened their blows. They did not take things as far as they could go. They knew enough to be afraid of cliffs. They understood that all pedestals were just pedestals— furniture pieces that could be remade every day. So when they told Kai sometime after his visit that they were separating, he was devastated but knew this thorn would leave a wound that would eventually scar over correctly. The news would not become a stubborn splinter that killed by infection. Kai's parents had become more attuned to the issue of dying as they aged, and there was no use in pestering them with tears if they no longer wanted to live with someone they had lived with for a long time. It was strange, but so be it. Not a puddle would widen. Kai, dry-eyed, accepted this crisis.

It was not strange that Kai knew little about his paternal grandparents. They had not been clever when it came to maintaining their son; they should have known better than to nettle the person their son married. Estranging one's daughter-in-law almost always guarantees losing contact with one's son. He will follow the person he chose. The parents of Kai's father had belittled his wife, thoroughly angering her, and so they saw their son very little afterward. He had gone to such lengths to win over Kai's mother. He would not lose her now. Kai's paternal grandfather had been an unsuccessful politician representing one of the southern provinces. His wife had been a college-educated homemaker who thought that her degree entitled her to make generalizations. It had been a mistake for Kai's mother to spend time with her in-laws so soon after her honeymoon. That was that.

When they passed away decades later, their eldest son, Kai's father, could not have been sadder. The collective voice of humanity, of everyone who had lost their own, spoke through him in his mourning: *I should have visited more*. His parents had both died from intestinal troubles, but was it a bad diet that took them or something else? Kai had wispy memories of a man sitting cross-legged, leisurely calling out to the children scampering around him, telling those little blubbies to come get candy and pocket money while his ill-tempered wife simmered nearby.

Once in a while, Kai's mother would begrudgingly acknowledge her mother-in-law's refinement. To have been educated in that day and age was no small thing. In the car while driving, she would sprinkle in such remarks. In the car, too, Kai's mother and father could become quite talkative. They would share their work troubles, troubling personal incidents, reactions to contemporary events, philosophies, disappointments, and triumphs. They blew the breeze back into each other, chatting about those who did not greet others properly, the rudeness of it all, how they themselves would not be so rude. Kai's mother would often become quite active in the car, covered in all her driving gear. She would don a sun bonnet, sunglasses, scarves, long-sleeved shirts, and driving gloves to keep out the sun, that soaring enemy, when it became insistent. If the sun turned nasty, she would not hesitate to clamber over into the back seat from the front while still shading her face with a brochure as Kai's father drove everyone to an early-bird special. If the sun overreached, so would she. This lovely woman would call Kai's father when Kai was hungry. These lovely people who cherished their children so much would rush off together with Kai to eat.

One thinks more and more about times gone by as one ages. How could Kai not think about where he had come from when he felt as though his life were over? His father embraced him. His mother embraced him as well, laughing and fussing. His father joined in on the fussing, which looked fun. He made the fun more fun by dancing a little jig around Kai, jiggling here, jubbling there, wubbling with glee everywhere because Kai had come home, the prodigal pumpkin returned, that hog's snout! *Kai, you look as ugly as ever!* He had so much fun teasing Kai like this, which prompted Kai's mother to occasionally interject, *Do not say such things. They hurt the child's self-esteem!*

Exclamations upon exclamations—a delightful reunion commenced. It was a pleasant atmosphere because Kai's parents were in good health and (to Kai's knowledge then) not planning on getting divorced. No one was having affairs; no one wanted to; work was going, going; dining was good; days of rest were even better. Touchingly, while unaware of the particulars, they wanted Kai to feel better so he would not be like this anymore. *Please be happy, Kai. Kai, our love, dove, be happy. Hurry and sink into your happiness, find yourself awash in it, that whirlpool, unhurried forever. Be moderate in your grief. Do not be like that.*

Entering their apartment, Kai put his bags away in a room that used to be another's. Days of quieter wallowing and rest followed. His parents found themselves facing an anonymity that seemed familiar, but was it? Kai, their spoiled puppy, shilly-shallied after them. He would watch them nap after their four o'clock dinners, which he also adored since he tended to get hungry earlier in the countryside due to the smaller portions his parents gave out at lunch. In their presence, he reverted to his childhood self, peevish and teething, impatience personified. Kai would whine for more rice wine at the grocery store. He would grumble about the nation's antiquated sense of nationalism (an insight Han would have been proud of). His parents would nod in sympathy without letting go of their own trepidations about burning flags altogether. Watching them rest as he worked from home at night, seeing their heads nodding, the crumpled way they rested on the couch, Kai wanted to lose consciousness. Everyone lived as houseflies do in this twilight porch called life.

Kai regretted how impatient he was with his parents all too often. Here they were, doing their utmost to cheer him up. And Kai was the same as he had always been: a selfish bleep. It was stupefying. He was abject enough to keep blaming his parents for his disappointments, a gesture as illogical as it was futile—as futile as a bee's attempt to avoid getting swatted by crawling under a table pane it cannot later escape; as futile as the sight of other bees piled up in the corner of a greenhouse's window, all dead.

No one, Kai's mother told him, *should beg for love. It does not work that way. The heart is not a feudal system.* Kai prided himself on his filial piety, but how often had he raised his voice regarding where and when to have meals, holding the elders hostage with his tantrums? How could he behave this way to people who left oversized umbrellas open in his bed to shelter his face from the morning sun while he slept? One day, Kai's father crept up to ask when he would be ready to leave the house, as Kai was holding the day back. He received a snarl for an answer, which he did not know hid Kai's anxieties. (Kai had been working all night on a letter to someone whose car bumper he had damaged.) When it came to tears, how many had Kai let flow in their presence? How many tears had Kai wrung from them in turn about mostly small things that could not be fixed in a short time? How much power did tears command in this family? As transcendent as his tears were for his parents, they had garnered nothing from the lover who had left Kai. But the hairdresser's tears did not work on Kai either. When one loses interest in another, no one's tears mean much of anything. Tears become just wastewater then, incapable of watering anything subtle.

Both Kai's father and Kai were thinking more regularly of these things, of tears and time. Kai knew his father was doleful about his hair feeling oily even after a wash. He blamed it on his age. Kai's mother added sadly that she was afraid of emitting distasteful body odors when she grew older. She admitted this worry as she was gagging on her toothbrush while brushing her teeth. Kai's family had the habit of pushing their toothbrushes far back enough in their throats to scrape their uvulas. Thoughts, reminiscences, dreams, ghostly voices—who knew the difference between any of these things these days?

Kai ground his teeth more heavily than ever while dreaming. In one dream, he awoke in his former one-bedroom after having written a long letter to someone while two versions of his mother were present, one bustling around the bedroom, the other in the kitchen. The lover who had left was there too. In the bedroom, Kai's mother was sitting at his desk, then hanging clothes in his closet. Her kitchen doppelganger was resting on a chair by the dining table. Kai's former lover fiddled with something in the bedroom before joining Kai's mother in the kitchen, where he assumed the role of a court jester. From the kitchen, Kai called out to his mother in the bedroom, walking toward her to find that succored feeling. Drifting into the bedroom, where she was still rearranging his closet, Kai went up to hold her as the kitchen dimmed, receding into extinction. He held her, calling her name over and over, mumbling about a spring that never dried.

Other dreams presented other doubles. Kai was driving a truck that was transporting both a treadmill and pensioners toward a dim outdoor space where other gym equipment was lying around. A graveyard mound was spotted, which belonged to a former lover of Kai's lover in this dream. Kai felt no fear, as the area, despite the mound's presence, resembled a basketball court or playground in broad daylight. Some hours later, as he walked a few paces to unlock a gate in order to leave (and who knew where all the pensioners had gone?), he sensed a presence. Kai sauntered forward to open the gate with a key, feeling something amiss. Whoever was there was not really all there. Suddenly, Kai felt someone's hands clasping the back of his neck and rubbing his belt, and he heard a voice rasping, *Can you show me something?* It was a portly lecher rumored to be locking away his victims in an attic before transforming into a woman and cannibalizing them. Kai shoved him off as the duo scuffled through the gate into a hallway. Kai saw window drapes. Moving his hands to caress them, he was unsure whether those hands were his own.

The scene changed. Kai was swimming toward a celebrity's mansion. The sidewalk had morphed into a swimming lane. He was now floating in Yoon's school field, an ocean expanse hedged in by sidewalks. Kai became aware that he was looking over some bushes at a group of carol singers on Halloween night. The backdrop reminded him of Chicago's nicer suburbs, as depicted in an

American Christmas classic about a boy left behind at home. An American movie star was sitting in front of Kai with a few of his drinking buddies, gazing at other costumed revelers. He turned around and caught Kai looking with wonder at the carolers, especially the one dressed as a pumpkin. He believed he had caught Kai in an unguarded moment, but Kai had known he was being watched. The actor came over, plumping down beside Kai behind the bushes, inquiring, *What do you need?* They stole beers from a house across the street, making their way down a lushly wooded hill. A cab went by. They were in it. Along with a few friends, they were going to see a theatrical production featuring an actor whose stage name was La Cocha Rocha. Kai's date admitted he did not care for the show or its roach actor. The show showed no effort. The crew headed into an alcove that looked out onto the 63 Building. A white woman across from Kai chatted with him about his career choices—how Kai had come to the capital because he wanted to, not had to.

Why would Kai not want to? He had caught a dragon, a lucky charm, in numerous dreams. One catch had been a nine-meter-long eel. He repeated this triumph in a river, with a fisherman to guide his search for a rare river dragon. Kai caught a fearsome one, laying it on the riverbank. Despite being tied up, it got into a fight with another dragon that Kai had laid out earlier. The early-bird dragon won the fight over the river dragon that was now a dog being mauled into a bloody pulp. The shame of not having been able to control this fight tarnished Kai's career as a dragon catcher. He lost yet more credibility as a clan leader at around the same time for failing to prevent his niece from wedding an ineligible young man by the same river where he had caught the rare dragon.

Kai became someone who everyone pitied. A child under his guardianship was taken away. Authorities eventually returned the child. In his eagerness to expedite this process, however, Kai said some stupid things that made him seem unfit to tend after his ward. This mistake slowed everything down. It was too bad because fifteen years ago, Kai had composed a well-received scholarly paper on life and death. But after this dragon fiasco and the ensuing series of hapless incidents, his papers dried up. Once the child was returned, Kai released a new physics paper, titled *The Cloud of X*. It circulated among readers as a torrential downpour began, which caused abnormal waves to crash upon the shore. The waves were deafening. Everyone lived on the beach. Everyone was reading as the storm grew stormier. Kai's party tried to get home safely, its numbers thinning as the Yellow Mountain loomed closer. Rain kept raining. Kai's paper earned a single coupon. A voice from everywhere and nowhere boomed, *Because of Kai, something is complimentary.*

Another voice mumbled, *What are you wanting these days?*

Kai answered, *I want you to beg as I begged, beg for forgiveness, clutching your chest as drops that are not water land on your back. Let me luxuriate in this feeling. Beg before the dark river, opening and closing all extant doors without moving. You may lose your voice, but even the hairdresser's throat keeps vibrating after she deflates.*

And what should I say? the mumbler rejoined.

The address of your grave.

Someone was drooling on a terrace as Yoon drove Kai to his house in another reverie. Better than any impoverished dockworker, Yoon shimmied up a frail wooden ladder to reach his third-floor apartment. Kai tried to follow suit but got stuck somewhere, falling off in the end. Why did Kai keep falling?

Another night, Kai's mother steered a jeep up a mountain road. It was a dark and snowy night. Kai, and possibly someone else, accompanied her. They saw trucks going past them in both directions. Units from the base camp were attempting to prevent the jeep from sliding off the mountain, digging trenches everywhere. Kai's mother ignored all this activity, speeding to reach the summit. The incline steepened. As the jeep fell backward, Kai slid out of his seat, dangling upside down. Hovering before this vertical drop, Kai was in awe of the beauty emanating from the ground faintly in sight. The jeep fell off the mountain at last. It and Kai's mother fell past Kai in the night. She was wearing a green duffel coat. Kai caught up with her, grabbing her and his father as the plummet went on. The trio fell past a cafeteria, sliding to a stop on a ski ramp. They were alive. Kai's eyes fluttered open in disbelief. He perceived movement behind their eyes as well. Kai awoke and immediately called his father.

Lucid dreams were the most frightening. Sleep paralysis episodes were dreadful. During college, Kai had hallucinated that his roommate kept walking back and forth between his desk and bed, faster and faster, turning into a blur before rushing up to where Kai was lying in his own bed across the room, hovering over Kai with such ferocious stillness. Kai's limbs always stiffened from the feet up before such visions would come. Shadowy fingers crawled over Kai's father's sleeping form as another version of himself snored in the background. Voices whooshed near Kai's face, breathing loudly. If Kai punched his legs before his paralysis fully set in, he could stave it off. If not, he was doomed.

Like a paper plane altering its course midflight, these memories swerved into others: playing with other children at a barbecue, running down the hill together in pursuit of butterflies. There were fond memories of fondling friends and being fondled at summer camps. One third-grade girl had mused about what would happen if she and Kai stayed behind the others to have sex before swimming with them in the afternoon. Would Kai like to see hers? She would show hers if he showed his. Nothing dramatic followed, only a pleasant recess. They went through the motions of doing it on a stairwell, aping it as best they could without succeeding. Kai could be sentimental about childhood.

When the smell of caramel wafted anywhere, it conjured up the memory of Kai's maternal grandfather's house. Kai might as well have never left that caramel house in spirit, being so childlike and pampered in the home of his own parents despite the family's fighting over missing objects, like that time after a scrapbook gifted to Kai from a Japanese woman he had cherished had disappeared one day, thrown out by his mother, Kai suspected, because she did not think that woman was good enough for him. It is a melancholic feeling when one does not know who to blame for such misplacements, this daily accrual of lost objects—when there is no one to blame, when air is not air, only salt water pooling, cells dying from dehydration in immutable isolation.

IV

THIS HAPPENED—HOW could it be like this? The day contains funny discoveries at times. Below is a note that Kai found as he was cleaning out his room in the countryside. He was deciding what to take back with him to Seoul, secretly most intent on finding a photo album that his Japanese ex-girlfriend had made for him. But he found this instead. It was a note that he had written to himself during his high school exam season, when he was around the same age that his father's friend had been when he expired from cardiac arrest.

Each line had been read aloud when it was first typed. Kai had crafted this note one line at a time over a period of twenty-eight minutes on a word processor. Rereading it, all of it, his initial feeling of boredom passed into something different. Repetition has a way of doing that. If an incantation is carried out in the right humor, it is absorbed from petal to stalk to bulb, its warmth spreading like clean urine. If it is not rushed, a new feeling overtakes the old. It is not like the panting that arises when one plays that game where the spaces in between one's fingers are stabbed as fast as possible with a penknife. It is a trance that only the boredom that is not boredom can bring.

Do not despair.
Do not despair.
Do not despair.

Do not despair.
Do not despair.
Do not despair.
Do not despair.
Do not despair.
Do not despair.
Do not despair.
Do not despair.
Do not despair.
Do not despair.
Do not despair.
Do not despair.
Do not despair.
Do not despair.
Do not despair.
Do not despair.
Do not despair.
Do not despair.
Do not despair.
Do not despair.
Do not despair.
Do not despair.
Do not despair.
Do not despair.
Do not despair.
Do not despair.
Do not despair.
Do not despair.

Do not despair.
Do not despair.
Do not despair.
Do not despair.
Do not despair.
Do not despair.
Do not despair.
Do not despair.
Do not despair.
Do not despair.
Do not despair.
Do not despair.
Do not despair.
Do not despair.
Do not despair.
Do not despair.
Do not despair.
Do not despair.
Do not despair.
Do not despair.
Do not despair.
Do not despair.
Do not despair.
Do not despair.
Do not despair.
Do not despair.
Do not despair.
Do not despair.

Do not despair.
Do not despair.
Do not despair.
Do not despair.
Do not despair.
Do not despair.
Do not despair.
Do not despair.
Do not despair.
Do not despair.
Do not despair.
Do not despair.
Do not despair.
Do not despair.
Do not despair.
Do not despair.
Do not despair.
Do not despair.
Do not despair.
Do not despair.
Do not despair.
Do not despair.
Do not despair.
Do not despair.
Do not despair.
Do not despair.
Do not despair.
Do not despair.
Do not despair.
Do not despair.

Do not despair.
Do not despair.
Do not despair.
Do not despair.
Do not despair.
Do not despair.
Do not despair.
Do not despair.
Do not despair.
Do not despair.
Do not despair.
Do not despair.
Do not despair.
Do not despair.
Do not despair.
Do not despair.
Do not despair.
Do not despair.
Do not despair.
Do not despair.
Do not despair.
Do not despair.
Do not despair.
Do not despair.
Do not despair.
Do not despair.
Do not despair.
Do not despair.
Do not despair.
Do not despair.
Do not despair.
Do not despair.

Do not despair.
Do not despair.
Do not despair.
Do not despair.
Do not despair.
Do not despair.
Do not despair.
Do not despair.
Do not despair.
Do not despair.
Do not despair.
Do not despair.
Do not despair.
Do not despair.
Do not despair.
Do not despair.
Do not despair.
Do not despair.
Do not despair.
Do not despair.
Do not despair.
Do not despair.
Do not despair.
Do not despair.
Do not despair.
Do not despair.
Do not despair.
Do not despair.

Do not despair.

Do not despair.

Do not despair.

Do not despair.

Do not despair.

Do not despair.

Do not despair.

Do not despair.

Do not despair.

Do not despair.

Do not despair.

Do not despair.

Do not despair.

Do not despair.

Do not despair.

Do not despair.

Do not despair.

Do not despair.

Do not despair.

Do not despair.

Do not despair.

Do not despair.

Do not despair.

Do not despair.

Do not despair.

Do not despair.

Do not despair.

Do not despair.

Do not despair.

Do not despair.
Do not despair.
Do not despair.
Do not despair.
Do not despair.
Do not despair.
Do not despair.
Do not despair.
Do not despair.
Do not despair.
Do not despair.
Do not despair.
Do not despair.
Do not despair.
Do not despair.
Do not despair.
Do not despair.
Do not despair.
Do not despair.
Do not despair.
Do not despair.
Do not despair.
Do not despair.
Do not despair.
Do not despair.
Do not despair.
Do not despair.
Do not despair.

Do not despair.
Do not despair.
Do not despair.
Do not despair.
Do not despair.
Do not despair.
Do not despair.
Do not despair.
Do not despair.
Do not despair.
Do not despair.
Do not despair.
Do not despair.
Do not despair.
Do not despair.
Do not despair.
Do not despair.
Do not despair.
Do not despair.
Do not despair.
Do not despair.
Do not despair.
Do not despair.
Do not despair.
Do not despair.
Do not despair.
Do not despair.
Do not despair.
Do not despair.
Do not despair.
Do not despair.
Do not despair.

Do not despair.
Do not despair.
Do not despair.
Do not despair.
Do not despair.
Do not despair.
Do not despair.
Do not despair.
Do not despair.
Do not despair.
Do not despair.
Do not despair.
Do not despair.
Do not despair.
Do not despair.
Do not despair.
Do not despair.
Do not despair.
Do not despair.
Do not despair.
Do not despair.
Do not despair.
Do not despair.
Do not despair.
Do not despair.
Do not despair.
Do not despair.
Do not despair.
Do not despair.
Do not despair.

Do not despair.
Do not despair.
Do not despair.
Do not despair.
Do not despair.
Do not despair.
Do not despair.
Do not despair.
Do not despair.
Do not despair.
Do not despair.
Do not despair.
Do not despair.
Do not despair.
Do not despair.
Do not despair.
Do not despair.
Do not despair.
Do not despair.
Do not despair.
Do not despair.
Do not despair.
Do not despair.
Do not despair.
Do not despair.
Do not despair.
Do not despair.
Do not despair.
Do not despair.
Do not despair.
Do not despair.

Do not despair.
Do not despair.
Do not despair.
Do not despair.
Do not despair.
Do not despair.
Do not despair.
Do not despair.
Do not despair.
Do not despair.
Do not despair.
Do not despair.
Do not despair.
Do not despair.
Do not despair.
Do not despair.
Do not despair.
Do not despair.
Do not despair.
Do not despair.
Do not despair.
Do not despair.
Do not despair.
Do not despair.
Do not despair.
Do not despair.
Do not despair.
Do not despair.
Do not despair.
Do not despair.

Do not despair.

Do not despair.

Do not despair.

Do not despair.

Do not despair.

Do not despair.

Do not despair.

Do not despair.

Do not despair.

Do not despair.

Do not despair.

Do not despair.

Do not despair.

Do not despair.

Do not despair.

Do not despair.

Do not despair.

Do not despair.

Do not despair.

Do not despair.

Do not despair.

Do not despair.

Do not despair.

Do not despair.

Do not despair.

Do not despair.

Do not despair.

Do not despair.

Do not despair.

Do not despair.
Do not despair.
Do not despair.
Do not despair.
Do not despair.
Do not despair.
Do not despair.
Do not despair.
Do not despair.
Do not despair.
Do not despair.
Do not despair.
Do not despair.
Do not despair.
Do not despair.
Do not despair.
Do not despair.
Do not despair.
Do not despair.
Do not despair.
Do not despair.
Do not despair.
Do not despair.
Do not despair.
Do not despair.
Do not despair.
Do not despair.
Do not despair.
Do not despair.
Do not despair.
Do not despair.

Do not despair.
Do not despair.
Do not despair.
Do not despair.
Do not despair.
Do not despair.
Do not despair.
Do not despair.
Do not despair.

You X!
You X!
You X!
You X!
You X!
You X!
You X!
You X!
You X!
You X!
You X!
You X!
You X!
You X!
You X!
You X!
You X!
You X!
You X!
You X!

You X!

You X!

You X!

You X!

You X!

You X!

You X!

You X!

You X!

You X!

You X!

You X!

You X!

You X!

You X!

You X!

You X!

You X!

You X!

You X!

You X!

You X!

You X!

You X!

You X!

You X!

You X!

You X!

You X!

You X!

You X!

You X!

You X!

You X!

You X!

You X!

You X!

You X!

You X!

You X!

You X!

You X!

You X!

You X!

You X!

You X!

You X!

You X!

You X!

You X!

You X!

x

x

x

x

x

x

x
x
x
x
x
x
x
x
x
x
x
x
x
x
x
x
x
x
x
x
x

So the words had been written. But were they believed? Would these words help Kai now more than they had when he was trying to test into colleges in the capital? Four years is and is not a long time to wait for someone. It is not the magical forty that the Hebrews had to endure as they shuffled cards in the desert. But it is twice the two-year term assigned to each Korean male for military service. Two times two is four. And four is the number of years Kai had waited before his vase inside had cracked.

Kai was in the mood to talk to Jung. Yoon was busy. Yoon and Jung were the only two who Kai could confide in, who Kai respected enough to take advice from. Yoon was in Okinawa visiting an aunt who was the granddaughter of one of the original royal retinue. Jung was around. She was busy with work, but she would still make time to help Kai see things for what they were.

Listening to Kai's gossip remained one of Jung's favorite activities, especially now that she had met someone serious and no longer could go on as many dates with different people. Work was getting harder. She had been promoted to senior manager. At this stage in her life, Jung was rolling up her sleeves, devoting more time toward what she felt was dignifying her life, concentrating it. For her, it was no longer enough to play. She wanted to craft the stuff of life as one would a garden or an oil painting, even though life tends to, she was well aware, feel insipid beside its idealized forms. Early middle-aged adults like her tend to bemoan their youth the loudest. The presence of some vigor within themselves makes its loss more piquant.

Kai could not predict what Jung would say. One can still surprise an intimate acquaintance, showing off new sides to oneself or creating more from scratch as time goes along. Kai was convinced that people could change, as he could see them changing all the time around him. Anyone can change if they feel strongly enough about what for. It is impressive how profoundly and often people can change if they want to. Or how they fail to if they do not feel the cause enough. If they do not want to, they do not, no matter how far others let go of themselves in anguish, deflating to their darkest core. No is no, not yes. Could yes ever stay yes?

One can wring oneself dry, crying like a child thinking about such things. When Kai grew exasperated with this atmosphere of stylized profundity, he smoked and watched movies and drank. And asked whoever he was with, *What do you want to eat?* This was his trademark question whenever Yoon was in a bad mood. Yoon would tell Kai during such moments, *I am not as nice as you think I am. I never was.* Kai would not say anything in response. He would just kiss Yoon on the mouth gently and ask him what he wanted to eat. Before this customary kiss, Kai would always give Yoon an unreadable look. (Was he looking at Yoon in the same strange way others kept looking at Kai, or was it something else?) After he drew back from Yoon's face, Kai would start tidying things around the room or studiously typing into his phone to smoothen the situation, make things feel natural again before finding the right moment to look up and ask, *So where did you want to eat tonight?*

SIMPLE—NOT COMPLICATED—reasons move people to do things. To flip the table at a family reunion, as they say. Simple things are what linger after everything else has gone, branding themselves into our memory. The pursuit of complexity is wrongly estimated by many to be a primary human motivation. This is a miscalculation. It is not the whale that undoes us but the grass. It is an icy walkway, a bathroom fall that ruins a life.

What was that simple, singular reason that drove Kai to Mount Jiri on a long weekend after visiting his parents? He had told his family beforehand that the point of the trip was to study the chemical phenomenon of pearls forming in the human body. After a person is burned to ashes, pearls or stones of calcium can sometimes be found in their gelatinous areas. There are a number of famous monks who are buried at Jiri with plaques set up in their honor, detailing the number, size, and shape of any pearls these monks left behind. Temple-goers used to think these pearls were proofs of piety. No one thinks that anymore. Human pearls are simply part of a physiological process like any other. Regardless, Kai had told everyone that he was going on a weekend pilgrimage to this region, home of the country's largest national park, to walk on mountainous trails over pebbles that looked like these fire-borne pearls.

Jiri is known for its delicacy of wild black boar. Kai had some the night he arrived. The hotel he selected was once magisterial, but it had faded into a dusty fishbowl located at the base of the Jiri mountain range, slightly past the park entrance on land gained illegally through the use of bribes back before Kai's birth. Still, Kai nurtured much nostalgia for this place. It had been a favorite family haunt. Kai's parents would reserve a studio, laying out everyone's mats in a row before the television set. The adults would drink beers and eat peanuts, amiably discussing the matter of when to rise for which activities. Kai was attentive if a movie was on, cranky if not.

That night, Kai ordered thin slabs of boar's meat to be grilled in the hotel restaurant. He was impressed by how dark it was, though it was not that late. The sun set early in the mountains. The restaurant reminded him of another restaurant, which faced a private detective agency named Spring Days, in Jeonju's hanok district. The agency's name made it sound as though it specialized in tracking down philanderers. It had been an amusing sight for Kai, who had been eating at a restaurant specializing in stone-pot rice dishes across the street. *Spring days in the countryside, one does not say ... And right across from one of the oldest eateries in the region. All this sense of history must inflame the locals.*

The black boar was very fine. Kai was hungry because the day had been taxing. Hours earlier, he had walked less than a mile uphill to the largest monastery near his hotel. To control its mice infestation, this monastery was overflowing with felines. Hearing its bell toll as a monk kept striking it with a suspended beam, Kai had the urge to smoke. So that is what he did. He smoked at this temple that held up its roofs with slightly crooked logs while the bell pealed out. At that temple located at the base of Jiri, what was Kai thinking as the monk rang the bell, as the bell continued ringing?

Its vibrations went deep, but there was nothing much to them. That was this sound's symbolic fullness. The feeling of nothingness was the cusp of it. There was nothing in particular to be remembered from hearing the bell ring as Kai's cigarette smoke seemingly endlessly dissipated. There was no face for whom the bell was tolling. The bell was sounding for no one. That was why the statue of the golden one was smiling. *Soon*, the bell promised Kai, *soon any memories of burning incense and icy tingling, of weightlessness compounded by the sensation of pearls hardening in one's thorax, will mist into nothing. All nothing!* But this nothing that encircles everything from the beginning will itself be something—or not. Is it enough to dissuade someone from sleeping until they die of starvation or from running out into oncoming traffic? Or from jumping from a high place, not aiming for the skies or sidewalks but for someone scurrying around below, a poor creature unaware that a big bird is falling? If it is not enough, the question will solve itself. People will either go on moving or suit themselves by stopping. Life does not transpire under coercion.

Kai was listening to the bell, thinking, *Stop reminiscing, deliberately working yourself into a nostalgic mood over the dead. These are irrelevant things. If you feel like you have lost everything, that nothing matters or makes you happy, it was all for nothing, then do yourself a favor and stop dawdling. If your life is over, get to it already.* These were the words the bell was imparting. They made Kai feel cheerful. That metal piece was such a vicious casket. It was funny. *I hear you, bell. If I do not want the elevator door held open, shut it snappily, snappily.*

An abrupt turn—*one of the reasons why Buddhism is slightly less popular in Korea than Christianity*, Kai speculated, *is because it does not force an eternal feeling upon its acolytes. Setting aside, that is, the practicalities of Christianity rendering itself more accessible— less remotely located, less solitary, emotionally hotter, more story- based—the revelations that Buddhism yields are trimmer.* (These were things Kai liked to think about when not working.) But Buddhism gave Kai such a wonderfully liberated feeling. If life does not seem worth living, walk away without taking others with you. How exhilarating to know that one can leave behind everything at a moment's notice without any fuss or the broader world ending! This feeling, for Kai, was real wealth.

But no matter, he had to go on living. Not because meaning- lessness makes its own meaning or because living is something to do, like dying. No, the last line of defense was his parents: they would be inconsolable. *How badly would they take it?* This was a question that was very unamusing, an itch Kai left unattended.

The only reason that society outlaws suicide for the young and healthy has to do with the narcissism running throughout big capitalism. The rich will not stand for losing their stooges, and parents do not want their miniature versions caving in. So children, poor ones especially, are burdened with the task of living in a plodding fashion as various religious leaders drive by in sports cars.

Interspersed throughout Kai's inner diatribes were prayers marked by their inconsistency. Inconsistencies were piling up even as Kai was contemplating dying. *When my parents go, I want to go too. Or if that is too frightening, I want us to stay here together without end. No one leaves. If the water is good, I want to drink from that spring before it pours me out. I want to cling till the bitter end. Let us never let anything go.*

Kai was the type to abandon all deities if they did not uphold their end of the bargain. If he had waited four decades to enter a land promised to him, and that promise was broken, that god would not be his god any longer. *There is too much inner resistance. That says enough.* Where had these words been spread? *I am feeling strange lately, not myself of late.* Lately, Kai was feeling strange. Kai had begun looking at himself strangely. He could understand why more people were looking at him strangely, the meaning of that look that had been unreadable until now. Kai's eyes would start watering uncontrollably. His speech was gradually slurring more and more. In these mountains, the sun set early.

The bell was still sounding. That was quite a monk. That monk still had the strength to keep hitting the bell for half an hour as the sun was setting. Kai resisted the urge to go inside one of the buildings lest he risk being admonished again for sitting on a cushion incorrectly. This was a shame, as Kai felt like kneeling. There was something about the act of touching the ground with one's forehead that felt gratifying. This pleasure was not indebted to a cosmic presence but the gesture's physicality itself. It was a pleasure that quickened the sense that no one can win everything. This new lesson brought by the bell was refreshing. It was simple and direct. Kai sat for fifteen minutes or so to hear this bell, all the while smoking in the cold, thinking.

Occasionally, other tourists would irritate Kai's sumptuous feeling by taking pictures obtrusively and loudly talking. Even locals who should know better did not abstain from these vulgar acts. One tourist commenced a video call with his son in front of the bell ringer, who was still swinging the hanging log in elegant figure eights. The tourist panned the phone around to show his son what he was missing, what the tourist himself was ruining. Kai was disgusted enough to get up and move away. He peered at the sky, the forests surrounding the temple, the pagodas, the statues, the stones, the steps, the closed coffee stand. They did not peer back. The monks who lived at higher altitudes had it easier in some respects. They were spared from having to accommodate these daily intrusions.

Maybe Kai had come to these mountains to find a fitting burial place. The obvious is often the answer. One desired a view before one finished it. Was that it? *Tell us what you are feeling*, people kept telling Kai. *Tell us, please tell us.* Then everyone stopped asking.

I do not know what it all was for. I do not know what I am working for. Someone I looked at all the time chose not to look at me anymore. The one who knew what I was to the core—still, he did not choose me.

Well, then! When Kai came back to the hotel for dinner, he spotted an eighty-something-year-old woman smoking. She had picked at the breakfast buffet in the basement that morning with him. Kai asked her, *Why did you not go where you said you would today?*

Why should I, she answered, *when I am going to end up in the same place again? I just came for the air anyway.* She took great puffs of her cigarette as she said these things, grinning toothlessly.

The next day, Kai resolved to visit a more remote temple, one of the farthest away. He was interested in feeling the mountain's pearls biting into his feet. Would that feeling, coupled with the cold, bring him the clarity that people like to associate with pilgrimages? What was he thinking as he was walking upslope? Snow was falling. The day was still dark because Kai had decided to be ambitious and embark at dawn, when night lamps on the hotel's driveway were yet shining. What a ghostly feeling. The darkness billowed before him. The dawn's grayness seeped into the snow slowly, the dimness barely abating because Jiri's forests are dense enough to prevent light from cascading. They pack the night away, hoarding it during the winters. Kai measured each step for fear of falling. There were stones to mark out the path forward, sometimes only notches on surrounding trees. Little had changed since he had come here as a child. There were no guardrails. If one went over the edge on a sharp turn, that was the end.

Snowflakes were tickling his cheeks. Their touch transported him back to that moment when he had sat on a stone staircase near Jiri's summit. The snow brought back that summer for Kai, those memories of himself staring into the clouds as others trudged by, irritated by his partially blocking the stairway. He had been sweating profusely then; whether more or less than on this day, that was uncertain. The snow was mingling with his sweat, which summoned the remembrance of summer days.

The cold grew sterner. The incline steepened. There were still a fair number of people in Kai's vicinity, mostly middle-aged women with permed bobs and walking canes. The snow was falling faster, more thickly, each particle thickening, contorting. It was not dancing or floating down but coiling into his nostrils. A light blizzard was forming. He had only walked three kilometers, and it was like this. The path was getting sludgy. Kai was not wearing hiking boots, just sneakers. These shoes were becoming soaked in their entirety, but he felt like walking on. He kept going. He opened his mouth to eat some of the blizzard before realizing it would be acidic and so hurried to shut it. There was nothing to quench his thirst since he had not packed anything. He had not been in the mood to be careful, had not been thinking ahead, which was a pattern with him. No proper shoes, no water, no provisions—nothing to taste save the frozen rain.

Kai had become thirst incarnate. He was so very thirsty, tormented by the sight of frozen water that could not be drunk. His toes had gone numb from the cold—how exciting. The flaming hunger for water, the sludge encasing his shoes distracted Kai from the climb ahead. There were kilometers left to go. Now there was no one accompanying him forward, only the occasional figure coming down the mountain, someone or another who had woken up at four or five at dawn to make the climb, returning in time for a warm breakfast. But because the blizzard was worsening, none ventured any farther at present. All were turning back. Kai felt exhilarated and not too worried yet. When he saw no one else around, either going up or coming down, then that would be troubling.

The incline was over forty-five degrees now on a stone trail that had replaced the original wood-paved one. Those who were descending were looking at Kai strangely. What, he wondered, was the look on his face? A whistling Kai shouldered on into the day that was turning reddish from the sun cutting through the clouds and snow. A haze was forming around his lips as his exhalations bled into the pinkish blur enveloping him. *I am walking it out*—but what was it that was trailing the Kai who was thinking this way? It was no longer anyone in particular. Was it time itself? Time's arrow whistled one way, melting the world as it went. The incline was sixty-five degrees now. Kai was crawling on his hands and feet around boulders and trees. He had met two people in the last thirty minutes. Both had warned him to turn back. He did.

But only when the second person, a fifty-something-year-old woman, looped back after a few paces to fetch him, yelling that he was being silly, that was enough now, there was nothing left to prove, who could be dressed so ridiculously, was that even a jacket, were those shoes? Kai could not win. So he laughed and acquiesced to this woman who would not let his jacket go and kept patting him downslope.

Kai followed this prattler back to his hotel, where she was also staying. They both headed toward the banquet hall that contained the breakfast buffet after drying off in their individual rooms. That morning was quieter than usual since it was a blizzardy weekday that was neither Christmas nor New Year's. The hotel had sunk enough from its glory days that its verandas sported mold, the café in the lobby was permanently closed, and the gift shop had wares on display without anyone being behind the counter to sell them. Two people manned the front desk. Both were bored and indolent. A humidifier was coughing away in the background. The karaoke rooms were lighted without anyone being present to allow patrons in.

Sitting in the near empty buffet room, Kai saw again the woman who had led him down the mountain, sitting with her companions. Middle-aged women in the mountains often travel in groups of at least three. *Why were you so stubbornly going up the mountain when you knew the weather was not right?* she asked him. Her friends, it was apparent, had been informed about Kai. Before he had entered the room, while he had been in the shower bringing himself to an icy peak with his hand, they had already been seated. They were eating in silence now, politely avoiding eye contact with Kai, curious but stoking their curiosity in a disinterested way. They were reserved before this stranger, not being the welcoming sort, but they were undeniably curious. Kai could feel it. They kept looking at him indirectly.

Kai's benefactress continued, *Why did you do that? It almost looked like you were going to start something.*

Kai answered, *I had someone to meet at the top. I promised to meet that person there, like in the movies. That person was walking to our meeting spot from another base.*

These words were unconvincing. In an era of mobile phones, who would travel separately to meet at such a distance on a wintry day? Friends would meet beforehand to make the climb together; and no one would wear sneakers in the winter. It was childish to want to appear hardened by the vagaries of life before custom-abiding strangers. Kai had wanted to be an eyesore to fellow travelers on the mountain that day. He had succeeded in a modest way. But this victory felt unpleasantly petty. What a pity. He had even stooped to wearing the hotel's unattractive indoor slippers since he had ruined his sole pair of shoes during the climb. How had it come to this: bothering random women who had planned on enjoying their weekdays together? Was Kai that starved for attention?

The women nodded in unison, nevertheless giving the impression that they thought his story was strange. Everyone kept munching. *Well, I am sure your friend did not go there today. You should call them and have them meet you somewhere else.* Kai made small talk as everyone finished their food. His comments were normal enough to not arouse further suspicion. No one looked at him strangely when they left, although he knew they would speak of him as someone strange when they were alone.

At least the room was emptying, thank goodness. It was not even ten in the morning. What should he do for the rest of the day now that he was snowed in and hiking anywhere was discouraged? He would go to a bathhouse—yes, that was it. But the hotel sauna was closed. Kai decided to drive to a nearby village. There was a public bath there, a proper one. There would be time to soak, to spend two or three hours dawdling before having a beer, then coffee as a cleanser. He would return to his hotel room afterward to watch television and more snow falling. His balcony offered quite a view despite being dirty and lacking privacy. Voices from neighboring balconies could be heard very clearly. So closely were the balconies arranged together that anyone could hear everything through their shut windows. Looking through his balcony doors, Kai could imagine himself floating outward and downward into the evening—or upward and sideways. Imagine if everyone were to walk out onto their balcony that night, ready to join the ascent or sink orthogonally. There was no telling where anyone was going. Everyone was waiting without hoping.

Before he knew it, Kai was chin-deep in hot water. It was funny: he did not remember having eased into the pool. The sensation of being enveloped by mist and churning water had jolted him into the understanding that he was at the bathhouse, sitting in an indoor pool bordering a glass wall that reminded him of his sliding balcony doors. Kai was steaming in water as it was snowing outside. How was it that he was alone there? It was such a view—the darkening skies, snow falling, water roiling, snow piling in the courtyard like the heavy smoke tendrils once ever present in his maternal grandfather's house. Why did the image of Kai's limbless torso floating in a cauldron, scalded to the bone, hover without warning before his eyes? But it did not perturb Kai too much. Kai's thoughts kept drifting.

As a small child, Kai had never had a woman look after him. No women were ever hired as babysitters. This was the wisdom of Kai's mother.

Middle school had been fun. There was heavy petting. It was nice walking to school, holding hands with friends.

Who had slapped whom across the face?

Who was getting spit on?

Why had Kai reveled in all that punching and cursing?

Whose body had thudded on the floor above Kai while he was studying in the basement of his college library? As the authorities were clearing the building, Kai had caught sight of that person's face. It bore an expression of surprise. Kai suspected that she had changed her mind midflight. Such deaths were typical of exam season.

What would Kai's last words have been if he had been in her place? *Is what I am feeling right now because I broke up with a Japanese divorcé on the second anniversary of her father's death?* (Yoon had told Kai that the divorcé was too ugly.) *Now I am as old as that divorcé was then and in a similar situation.*

Is this compensation for disappearing from the lives of an anonymous many?

Is this punishment for striking my brother when we were young, for making him beg outside my door for me to play cops and robbers with him? How could I have sent that darling to the hospital twice for stitches?

Is this justice for fellating a college friend's ex-lover a year after their breakup?

Is it karma for tempting others to call me, only to humiliate them over the phone once they do?

Is this for the hairdresser?

Or for how I treated my mother and father?

Is it for organizing a ring to stonewall a certain fifth grader when I was the same age because she was slightly dumpy and too eager to please?

Is this for cheating?

Am I a hyena or a zebra running the wrong way? This must be overdue retribution for being both the lighter and the flame. The great Kai is reduced to garden fodder. 'Tis the season for jolly locusts, truly.

Kai started smiling. The warm water infected him with another vision, one that genuinely thrilled him and made him afraid. He was placing his hand over a running gas cooker. *What a fun game*, Kai could see himself thinking in the scene. Suddenly, Min was setting him on fire. An entire apartment complex burned to the ground after Min made his escape. What Min would never forget in prison, however, was the memory of Kai roaring with laughter. Kai was smiling as he was being immolated. The image of himself being flayed by Min's reedlike hands hung over Kai in the pool where he rested. It was time to arise and either dip in the cooler pools or sit in some steam room before scrubbing his grime out with mitts. Kai stood up. He walked a few paces, performed a few ritual stretches, steamed, dunked, and rinsed in preparation for the scouring. No one else, it seemed, was coming in that day.

It was eerie in the empty bathhouse, but Kai eased into the space. The day had only just settled into the afternoon. Kai was being overly sensitive to the sound of pitter-pattering after having faced down the mountain. Would he dream that night that dream of being rocked on a boat by a faceless darkness that murmured, *It will be all right. We are here where we are. Hello, Kai.*

Kai giggled like a kindergartner as bubbles rose to the surface. *I am an unhappy person. My unhappiness all too happily grows with time.* Alone in the bathhouse, he sobbed with a pain not too dissimilar from the hairdresser's pleasure. Like her, he sobbed with his lips utterly compressed. His agony never escaped that clenched mouth, concentrating in his throat, a fist of vibrations, of muted wailing.

Hours later, late that night, Kai would go to sleep, lulled by his stomach's growling. Until then, keep scrub-a-dub-dubbing. Rubbing off one's own film of dead skin did not instigate an inward purging. It was merely a mechanical process to prevent Kai from feeling moist flakes of himself peeling off when he scratched his heels together. Why was Kai wearing his locker key around his wrist when no one would steal it were he to put it down? The baths were deserted. Kai kept forgetting it was a weekday in the middle of winter. The mitt that Kai was holding as he stooped down to sit on a plastic chair appeared friendly to him. Kai waved to his image in the mirror with it. How peaceful it was. As he could see through the glass, the snow had not ceased falling. Kai did not feel like investigating the outdoor pool, which was closed. Or did he? He did.

Who am I friends with? I feel as though I am friends with nobody. Was I friends with the one who left? I think so. That must be why I am disoriented. We were not friends before, but we became friends as we became lovers. That is why the bye-bye feels more bitter.

Kai reminisced about friendship as he drove back to his hotel over slippery roads. The snow was not several meters deep. It was only a few centimeters high, still soft enough. Nevertheless, Kai drove carefully. The day had not made it past the late afternoon.

In the evening, Kai looked for stars from the parking lot. The air was exceptionally crisp. It was a night rare to find these days, the acidic snow having purified the air, acting as a blotter. Kai wanted to look twinklingly upward. That wish was thwarted. There were not that many stars observable, even deep in the Jiri mountains. There were no stars to make poetry out of. A few twinkles here, a few twinkles there—Kai started grumbling, feeling baleful. *Those twinkles are looking down at me from an unimpressive sky. Are the stars pure or corrupt or nothing much of anything?* To be corrupt was easy, but Kai wanted to be pure like his mother's sleep-talking. *Stop, dear time, so these figures huddled near me, nosing their pillows, do not melt away into transparency.*

What was it that kept Kai awake that night? The mat felt thinner, as though it had shrunk. The floor crunched into his spine. The ground reminded Kai that it was there and unyielding. His back was aching. The room was dim. A moon that was not full shone through half-drawn curtains. The windows were closed to keep warmth in. Kai stirred on the floor, but that was not the same thing as being stirred. It was not the heat that kept open his eyes. It was not the room's stuffiness.

Something was thrumming. It was not white noise. It was— what was it? The mat might as well have been absent. The television had only a few channels available. Kai was unwilling to pay this hotel for subscription erotica. Hard-core amateur videos online won out over the soft-core professional variety on most days anyway. While the floor was warming nicely, it was time for Kai to push off his duvet. He was not perspiring.

An hour later, his breathing was slowing. Kai sat up, scratching his scalp. That no one was in the room with him was a blessing, the heft of his breathing being inexcusable. There is nothing worse than loud breathers, especially of the congested variety. Big, big breathers do not care how their gulping infuriates others. Kai was being such a breather in that instant. Kai was sighing obnoxiously enough to be just shy of groaning. Enough was enough: he rolled over and went to the lobby. It was not more of the starless night that he was hunting for but a place less claustrophobic than his bedroom. Was there somewhere to rest from thinking?

Sitting in the darkness near the hotel's glass doors that opened out onto a series of rusted terraces was soothing. The night was lovely, and sitting there like that gave Kai a quiet, holy feeling. The dark converged with moonlight and empty space. It felt like the world at large was empty save for himself in this crumbling kingdom past everything.

But what was it that was shimmering in the lobby with him? Who was there? As Kai was sitting, a breathless sensation broke over his body, the same he experienced whenever great mists erased the shore behind. There was someone else there with him. Kai was being watched from somewhere. But who—what—was looking, tensing? The thrumming in his ears became the sound of a train entering a tunnel. A presence as translucent as his reflection in a train window stared back at him. It was tenuous yet tangible, like a raindrop hitting the pane. There are many legends dedicated to the ghosts of students who kill themselves at school, all from the race to perform favorably on the nation's university entrance exams. What had happened here at this hotel?

It was Kai staring. The spectral wisp was another Kai who was not a reflection. Or was it his reflection, a starlit Kai in the glass, an image like one glimpsed in a subway's platform screen doors? Kai breathed out noisily again: *I have come to the end of myself. I need to stop drinking. What is that?* It was Kai, and Kai was it, sitting there so sadly, a faint torso that upheld a head that turned toward Kai when Kai turned his. As in certain sleep paralysis episodes, the future was collapsing into the present. The future was receding, a wave without an ocean.

What was Kai to make of this vision? He convulsed awake at around noon the next day. The balcony was snowed in. Everything outside was blasted in whiteness. There was no memory of how he had fallen asleep or how he had returned from the lobby. Who could say whether he could say with any confidence that he had not fallen asleep in the lobby? He may have never left his room to begin with.

No, these are not real questions. They are tame and affected. Everyone knows when a dream is a dream and when it is not. Its qualitative experience needs no explaining. Kai could not sleep, so he had wandered into the lobby. He was lying when he told himself that he could not remember how the night culminated. Kai had seen or felt something in the lobby and darted back to his room, locking the door and windows, closing the curtains, turning the lights on, turning the television on to some cooking channel, huddling under the duvet, making an extra cocoon for himself with the floor mattress, backing up against the wall, and watching the screen while straining to hear any footsteps in the hallway. The strain lessened as the night deepened until Kai, quite worn out, had turned off the television and lights and went to sleep, buried beneath his covers, sealing his hair and toes from what would seem to be the air itself.

Taking in the view from his noontime balcony, Kai vowed that he would not think about what had happened in the lobby last night. The event was too terrible to mull over. Kai would forget it all. He would not bother going into acts of exegesis. What had happened was not possible. That was what hallucinating felt like. The imaginary did not mean anything. Yesterday night had unfolded like a dog's dream, proverbially speaking. But Kai had never been confident about that proverb's meaning, about whether it gestured toward the dream nonsensical enough to belong to a lower life-form or so infuriating to its dreamer to render them rabid.

NO ONE COULD find Kai's brother. Where was he?

HAN SLEPT WITH my wife! This was the cry that pealed out in the United Nations village. That village crier knew that there is some loneliness attached to getting on a train and then off it without feeling altered. A train can become a spiraling staircase with dimly lit snow at the bottom. Was Han on a train, or was his train of thought splintering under the pressure of his wanton dream states? Sadness can spread from one to another, from an undreaming body in bed somewhere to one moving up a frozen mountain to another drooping on a couch, wilting in torpor, dreaming of that infamous line of sheep losing its formation before the mind's eye. Had Kai's sadness infected Han?

Han was in trouble as the snows thickened. The more broadcasts that aired regarding a snowstorm's inconveniences, the deeper the furrow in Han's brow grew. A troubled Han was on a train from Seoul to Busan. He had prescribed a ginseng mixture to the Korean wife of a white American sergeant, one who had been trying to conceive for three-quarters of a year. She had reacted badly to the tonic, enraging her husband, who was now threatening Han with a lawsuit. Han could see this situation becoming messy.

Han eventually overdosed on heroin. It sounds incredible, but this is what happened.

People like doing things for the sake of doing them. It does not mean they have given up on life or care about nothing. It does not need a deeper reason other than a certain momentary pleasure:

a sharp quivering that swells, some succor. There is so little relaxation in this world that urges everyone to work without rest for its luxuries (and workers cannot pretend anymore that they can do without them; that time is past) and that instills the belief that whatever happens to others elsewhere will not happen here. *No one could be so careless*, those right here think to themselves. *The numbers are too ridiculous for our names to come up.*

Han would go from heroin. This is what happened before he left.

The fallout with the sergeant's family was not to blame for Han's drug habit. It had started before then. The stress caused by the legal dispute did, however, take its toll.

The rumors swirling around Han's rise and fall would be so numerous that his actual story became very confusing. But Han would die of heroin, that was certain. What happened before then was that he had become entangled with a woman who had been coming to him for months to help her get pregnant because she and her husband, not a sergeant but a lieutenant colonel from Tennessee, were having difficulties building their family. She had tried expensive hospital treatments but figured that it could not hurt to test herbal remedies as well. She had come in. She was not pretty, although that does not mean she was homely. She told Han her refrigerator was stocked with Aronia berries and noni juice, her being disciplined about these things, yet the seed would not take root.

Are you having regular relations with your husband? Han had inquired.

Yes, scheduled during my ovulation period, yet why do my periods keep coming?

Han looked at her slower. Something about the way she was answering his questions was attractively demure—was this quality sincere?

On her end, she saw a self-important rooster who talked a few seconds too long at each measure. Whatever happened to Han? Why had he faded away from some white powder? He was tall, but he may not have been as tanned and jollily jowly as his acquaintances had long perceived him to be. (Kai, among them, had felt from the beginning that Han had an instinct for teasing people about their hypocrisies without ending his friendships with them. Han knew how to tease people and put them in their place and have their thanks for it. If someone said anything that contained the slightest drop of much too serious disingenuousness, Han would say, *What about it, darling? You made a greater racket over much less, would you not say? Come, come now, what is this? Did so-and-so sleep with your wife or husband? What is this really about? Tell me, I am dying, crackling with curiosity. Did they do something to you? Were you stomped on?* The Han of such talents was lost to Kai; and Kai remained at a loss over how to publicly articulate his surprise over Han's passing.)

What was known was that the colonel's wife resembled her husband's ex-lover. Before the colonel became her husband, he had been a lower-ranking officer sniffing around to see if this woman who looked like the other one he had wanted to marry but could not (because her parents had refused to give their blessings) would say yes to him. He had wanted her to say yes to and for him, on his behalf before the world. The colonel often had to say no to everyone and was sagging from it. When he met his future wife—a woman who was not the woman he really loved, only looked like her—he was living like a bachelor's bachelor. He would come home to a sparsely furnished apartment that smelled sour from male perspiration, with nothing in the fridge and a friend or two in tow from the workplace—men who enjoyed competing and testing one another for weaknesses.

All this had become tiring. Conversations regarding how well everyone was acclimating to Seoul were the most tiring.

To his wife, the colonel was kindly. He tried to be as conscientious as possible about not overstepping his place, even as he could not entirely escape the conviction that he was part of the arm of global security and democracy in a land wavering in both. The two had met in a bar. She was a blue-collar receptionist who did not see him as a nice prospect. At least, though, he had not been sexually aggressive but patient and chaste in the way he approached her. He remained sober that night, knowing himself unable to take to alcohol very well. Their match was typical for marriages between American officers and Korean women. The kind of woman who would marry an American military man would rarely be upper-middle-class or above, physically attractive, unselfconscious, and uneager to please. All this is what Kai, not Han, believed. Han more or less agreed, but the tenor of his pronouncements regarding such intermarriages was less harsh. Life has a way of bringing people together.

Right when Han was teetering in his office that increasingly felt like a chicken coop, where the clients crowding in day after day were bores, hypochondriacs, perfectionists, or solipsists, he met someone as equally worn out as him. The colonel's wife confused Han for the pleasure she took in lording her station as the wife of a lieutenant colonel over the other army wives on base.

Was it that special, Han wondered, *when marrying a foreigner was not necessarily something to be proud of?*

She said during her first meeting with Han, *My husband and I are having trouble conceiving.*

I see. What medications are you taking?

She was not lisping as she listed them out, but her tongue came up ever so short. It was charming. They began an affair.

Or was the colonel's wife too uninventive to imagine doing that sort of a thing? Despite what certain books and movies show, it takes courage to embark upon an extramarital affair. Men usually have to be insistent and women alluring enough to work their admirers into that state, to encourage them to make the effort and risk rejection. Women do not, in general, have the nerve to take the initiative.

The colonel's wife was anxious to do well in her marriage. She was proud of her husband's achievements, a territorial hen among other army wives, with long, undyed hair that was permed straight, her single vanity since she did not have the discipline to exercise routinely nor the genes to eat in an undisciplined fashion.

No one knew how far things went between her and Han, or why. Han was a droll one, a wire surging with bon mots. The mouth that turned risqué when not ranting could be calm and dispassionate, a goody-goody doctor's mouth. He could have had anyone he wanted if he were not so distracted. He made a good living. Why was he drawn to this woman whom he himself considered to be a few dozen cuts beneath him? Was it for the same reason that Kai was drawn to the hairdresser: being stirred by someone who was unthreatening and deferential? Or was it because of the soft, nobly pitiable air the colonel's wife shrouded herself with as she told her story about wanting a child but not being able to have one? It was appealing for Han to see her dejected because she was so for charming reasons: she wanted a son who would not be drafted into any army (but go of his own accord if that was what he wished) or a daughter who would be more attentive and inclined to call home often instead of simply leaving and becoming distant when she started taking college classes.

The colonel was distraught, though. Not only was a child not coming, no matter what mixture his wife drank, her breath stinking as she exhaled at night, but the atmosphere on base these days was funny. The clean-minded one from Tennessee was worried. The number of troops on the peninsula was shrinking. This winter was the worst. The administration had changed in America; corresponding changes were happening on the peninsula. The direction of these collective changes was unclear. It was unclear whether things were heading toward something along the lines of: Koreans should be footing the bill for Korea, North Korea is too much of a threat, North Korea is not enough of a threat, Japan will neutralize any threat, Japan itself is an ongoing threat, or what can neutralize China? The colonel had heard whispers that more American units were to be sent away in the spring. So what was what—what was happening? Things were all the more erratic since American leadership had reshuffled while China was growing.

After having said goodbye to his wife in the morning, the colonel walked to his work compound. He imagined that she would go about her day by consorting with other wives, going to Han, cleaning the house, getting groceries, and walking their dog. In reality, he did not look into what she did when he was away because she was so placid. The details did not matter or were untroublesome. Snow was falling. The air felt thinner. It was not a drone in the distance—ah, snow, crunching beneath his boots. The guards by the gates saluted him.

The problem was not so much about an affair gone wrong or Han's professional ennui escalating but the mood that was brewing on the peninsula. The sun sets early in the mountains. Did that mean it would set early on the mountainous peninsula? The colonel's second-in-command was walking toward him. She told him, with a look full of suggestiveness, that it was not looking good. A clash might be coming.

The colonel stiffened. *She does not believe what she is saying. No one does.*

How could another war erupt given the millions living in Seoul, the quality of life there, and the fact that no one in North Korea would start such a thing? To do so would invite ruin—not a wall being knocked down but the collapse of an entire country. If nuclear warfare happened, there would be no going back for the North Korean nation. The whole world would send its troops in, and North Korea would become a territory that Americans, Chinese, and South Koreans squabbled over as Russians looked on. No one believed that North Korea would actually do something unless the universe was not this universe and gravity was not gravity. In that other cosmos, life would not be favored over death. That being said, Mister Jowls could push a button knowing that it was his last move; there would be no other. The mad always overreach. Napoleon and Hitler liked throwing rocks at Russia, Alexander would not sit still, and Japan destroyed Pearl Harbor knowing how furious that would make the Americans, who became awash in the blind rage of a husband used to beating his wife but turns around to find that same wife cursing and spitting at him. Murders happen in these cases when spirits find those they deemed their social inferiors daring to revolt. The colonel was worried that the unthinkable could happen if the meatball thought he had nothing left to lose in the corner he was backed into. But he was not yet backed into a corner. The situation was nowhere near unsalvageable. None mistook this one for Genghis Khan.

But what if? That *if* always gets us. So many strange things had been happening lately, one never knew. It was not that things were getting worse over time as they were getting better on the whole, certainly better than when none of the comforts of modern living existed and the acts of mating and giving birth were full of risk. Things were certainly better now than when warfare consisted of cleaving lumps of flesh off a body with skillet bits, just knifing others in broad daylight before a public resting on a grass knoll. Were people bored enough to want to touch lava rising in the heat again?

The colonel was not an alarmist or a jingoist. He could be as cool as any Korean cucumber in ignoring all the bells and whistles around. He knew no nuclear bombs were going to drop. The North had been threatening to trigger a sandstorm for decades. So why were there so many huddled conversations and glances thrown everywhere?

The colonel was not naïve enough to think that a war would soon be forthcoming. Or that his government was above any and all questioning for the direction it had taken things. He could understand more than ever why the locals could be unfriendly. It was just that no one likes to be the frog trapped in a pot, surprised by its surrounding waters boiling slowly.

The colonel was a thinking man in the army. He was a blond with blue eyes and not of the same ilk as those bad-apple missionaries back at Yoon's secondary school. The colonel was slightly provincial, there was no escaping it, but he was not proud of it, did not glory in it, was not corrupted by it, was not wounded in it, and was not goaded into spitefulness as a result. There was no fear of being condescended to in him. He was above patronizing other people, minus in the universal sense that no American can escape when, as Han claimed, an American goes somewhere that is not Western Europe, Scandinavia, Finland, Iceland, Greenland, all the cold lands, England, or Canada. He was kind and did not play up his Tennessee drawl. He spoke a nicely bland, educated English in an alto voice sounding from an unmemorable face.

And he would think to himself, looking at his wife sometimes, that Koreans were like greedier Americans, being afflicted by a sharper loss of leisure and deep culture, scrambling for money as they did without showing any manners. No one held the door open for anyone. All this fighting over nothing. Did he want to have a child here? The child would eventually be taken back with him to the States. The little junior certainly would not be permanently raised here given how the colonel had not grown to love the peninsula as he loved his own country. The peninsula was not shrouded in romance for him. It was a tiring place for him. He and Han were unwitting brothers in their sharing of this feeling.

The colonel's wife's barrenness put a strain on her marital relationship. The husband doted on her in a straightforward, earnest way. His love was monogamous, satisfied with itself. There are people like that who do not look at other people after they decide to formalize their feelings through marriage. Settling down for them means settling into a way of experiencing. These husbands may peek at pretty women with toned bodies in scanty clothing on the street but never for more than a second and with any serious intent. These glimpses are merely glimpses into a world none of them would enter even if given the chance. They would not take it because they would not believe it was real. This chance is not a part of their world or psychological constitution.

For the colonel who had come to Korea to serve his country and see a bit of the world as a bonus, did his wife need some comforting words to bring the pressure down? Perhaps a baby would come faster if he gave her more verbal placebos, saying the same thing in different ways to make her feel better even if that was not what he felt or believed. What could he say? *We do not have to have one right now; we can also adopt. Actually, we do not have to have one at all.* He said these things to her, and while his wife appreciated the lip service, the way he ordered his sentences aggravated her. The option of not having one was offered as an afterthought. He wanted a child—probably more than one since he came from a big family.

But what had this to do with Han and his dying prematurely? Why was Han involved with a couple who could not conceive, with the wife coming into his office at least once a week, her features twisted from her heavy sweating and internal cramping?

It turned out that the couple later had a child. Han was not told whether it was a boy or a girl (and he was too tired to ferret out this information), but the colonel's wife rolled over the babe in her sleep soon afterward, specifically while nursing it half-upright in bed. Might she have rolled over it because it looked like someone who was not her husband?

Han never came to know that the colonel and his wife lost their firstborn in this way. He only knew that the wife who had frequented his office eventually became pregnant and that the child may or may not have been his.

All that anyone could say was that the colonel was treading water in a pond full of whisperings, of whispers that trouble was coming. The snow was coming down harder. Something in the fallow earth was thickening, shifting. Plate tectonics were creaking into unknown formations. Han felt as though he were locked in a panic room at his office. The same physiognomic types kept peopling his hallways, such human nothings making Han's life feel like nothing, so very boring. The young would arrive for their tonic prescriptions that would help them do better on their exams or general office work, with an eye toward moving up the bureaucratic ladder, which would help them secure lovers with greater success. Older patrons would come in for various pains across their bodies, as they were wobbling under time's duress, their spirits correspondingly flagging. The yet more aged wanted respite or maybe just a clean, well-ventilated place to rest.

Younger or older, it did not matter to Han anymore. It was the same story of having to fix a car in a chicken coop, with sullen, pockmarked nurses scraping around in rubber slippers over white socks. The money was not bad. Women and beady-eyed relatives were ever present, waiting for crumbs from Han's expensive tables. The colonel's wife did not snoop around anymore. She was set—good for her. The subjects she mentioned that her husband was preoccupied with these days were unsettling, but they did at least provide something to think and talk about during meal breaks. Han began self-prescribing stronger doses of ginseng extract while drinking steadily, a combination he forbade for his patients, as the alcohol would not only negate the cordial's effects but work against them, turning everything into poison inside one's gut. Alcohol mixed with herbal medicine turned acidic. There were no more women in Han's schedule. Han was too tired of the predictable. It was now just Han and his work cupboards.

Along with spiking both his gin and ginseng tonics with soju, Han fell into a heroin habit. His high school and college acquaintances spread the word that his death was a movie star's. So deft was he at administering his doses that his powder boiled on his spoon in exactly the way that one sees in movies. *What a lower-class black problem, nay, even an increasingly middle-class white problem to have in upper-class Korean society,* they told one another. *Quite glamorously surreal, really.* The Han who lived by the river went out in a blaze of disreputable glory while working as an herbal specialist.

Han's life may have been boring, but his death certainly was not. It gave his friends, family, acquaintances, and patients something to talk about for many years afterward, being the gift that kept on giving, a volcano that would not stop trickling out an excited, abstract feeling.

There should be more heroin on the peninsula. Han is a hero, some might say. *Why is it frowned upon? So what if everyone lives longer and more productively? Such a phenomenon would be useful for whom and what? Big companies—is that it? It would be nice if heroin snowed down on the peninsula, piling several meters high so everyone could skip work that week.* Han would have had fun with this rhetorical tactic, of using himself as a case in point for finding a better work-life balance and expanding civil liberties. There would be none to match him.

Han became intimate with a woman he was incompatible with, bending his life toward a man he had more in common with. Did Han know the colonel personally? Had they ever met, crossed paths? Did he like the colonel as a human being because both lived where they did not prefer to, yet when they tried to live where they thought they belonged, it did not feel right? When the colonel cruised along a highway that bordered the American South (with his wife in the front seat or absent altogether), he had the same unpleasantly anonymous feeling that Han had when he traveled in Europe.

Han was gone from a residential area located south of the Han River. Around the time he left for good, Han could and did sit for hours in his bedroom, experiencing time in shrapnel form: its units became his labored breathing and phlegm-filled coughs in a darkness that alternated with light in a box sealed by shutters. *The other room without walls outside of this one is more alike than different from the latter,* Han had been thinking. *It is the same leaf turned over at dusk during scything season. The ancients discovered that they and everything else still disappeared with the mountains after the old prophets, pamphlets, and miracles had been hung up to dry. None walked on water or heard anything in the dunes, yet even if they had, we would feel the same.*

Toward the end, when Han was letting himself go to seed by making too much of a transparent effort, he was convinced, to not scare off others through his emaciation, slovenliness, excessive throat clearing, and dark circles, his own lack of emotional flexibility had begun to bother him. Han felt himself to be too emotionally brittle and that that may have been the reason for his discontent. One must be a little adaptable to keep going, not brittle and insistent on maintaining all the trappings of one's personal triumphs. Be like the simpletons, moochers, brawlers, and feckless who live hand to mouth every day for coarse, hearty pleasures, all kept afloat by an astonishing life force.

Before he overdosed, by accident or on purpose, Han would periodically attain calm through thoughts of how there is not necessarily any traditionally profound interior or exterior to anything. Everything can be anticlimactic. Everyone wants their life and death to mean something, but nothing does. That is why suicide can be an easy and comfortable course of action, as cozy an act as shaving a pencil or plucking a hair from one's chin. A cold bead forms in one's gut as one thinks to oneself, *Am I really going to do it?* The earworm becomes a vague agrarian impulse to be at one with the earth and maggots. One's flesh sinks to the level of a rodent's, with fur and cartilage welding together into a board that grows soggy. That bead of coldness inside one's stomach is very cold indeed, lowering in temperature as it contracts.

What was happening physiologically to Han during his last days was like the sensation of following someone's back through a crowd with the inevitability of a movement that comes to fruition over years. It can take years to muster the courage to follow someone like this, much in the way it does to declare a venerated tree very, very dead and remove it from the property as a consequence.

This is not it. A change is needed.

Years before Han took his own life, or overdosed, or treated both as synonyms, he had a dream about a friend who snubbed him. This friend had dared to rent a whole studio to himself beside the apartment where he and Han still rented two nonadjacent rooms out of the four available, meaning that there were two other roommates present. Han had woken up yelling for he had been admonishing his friend while asleep. How could he have done this? If he had had the money this whole time, why had he not told Han so Han could help him move out and find an appropriate two-bedroom together on that same budget, sparing Han from having to continue living in such a hovel? What a waste of money. Han's friend had instead rented himself a shabby studio in addition to his original room in the four-bedroom apartment, the latter of which was not even located next to Han's room, so Han could not conveniently use it as a study or fitness center in his friend's absence. Feeling his neck muscles and forehead veins bulging out like hog bristles as his cheeks turned crimson, Han screamed and screamed himself hoarse for what he perceived to be an act of extraordinary selfishness when it meant nothing. In the waking, more rational world, why should Han's friend not rent out a studio if he wanted to and escape the hassle of finding a new place with Han when he had done Han a favor already by moving into that unattractive apartment in an equally unattractive neighborhood solely to be closer to Han and so water their friendship?

Even his decision to stay in Han's vicinity by additionally occupying the studio next door instead of moving somewhere else entirely without Han was a good-humored gesture. It had not sacrificed physical proximity and still subsidized Han's rent by dividing his household's total by four instead of three.

Some of Han's memories assumed a dreamlike sheen. One of his favorite memories to share at parties was the story of his being caught in traffic one summer day with an imported car in front of him and not a few drivers standing around, fighting like one of the late-middle-aged waitresses working at a shellfish broth shop in Busan who enjoyed day drinking, became abrasive while doing it, and had a habit of cursing at her customers whenever her broth became good and ready. Not toward any table or individual, as that kind of particularity could provoke a fistfight, but at the room in general, diluting the insult enough so that no one and everyone felt stung simultaneously. *Jesus in hell, let us eat*, she would bark once the restaurant's volume reached a certain point, referring to herself and the rest of the staff who wanted to take a break and eat the shop's food instead of serving or cooking it.

Few knew that Han had abhorred and cherished everything at once, having translated the world into a series of unpublished stories kept on an off-brand laptop tucked inside a medicine cabinet at his clinic.

When he had not been losing control of himself in a discreet way, Han had been writing. He had begun writing so as not to forget his dreams upon waking. If he turned over and fell back asleep without recording what he had experienced during his slumber, he would not remember anything for posterity.

Perfecting his pastoral descriptions had become one of his passions as he grew more attentive toward the task of dream worldbuilding. The challenge was that he had not cared about what objects looked like in a painterly sense, remaining uninspired by light flickering across bodies of water, indifferent to how it refracted and sharded out across a horizon. Light on water invoked tortuous analogical chains wherein water stood in for everything that was not itself due to its seemingly boundless figurative qualities that rendered it more amorphous than it already was. Water was never water but a byword for something else. Water was more watery than common sense would allow. Water was murkier than light.

These were the kinds of abstract introspections that were not appealing to Han. When someone is depressed or both clumsy and unlucky with their substance use, who cares what the world looks like? So Han was not an adept recreator of tableaux even as he was fond of the dream world to which they belonged, dealing with exterior details more or less as a visually impaired man would, like he and these details were two ships passing in the night.

As a partial solution to this dilemma, Han inventoried what was present in his dreams with great vigilance while glossing over their optical particulars, which were too many and difficult for him to describe. His inventories of props, actors, and backgrounds amassed in size while making no equivalent strides in qualitative depth. These qualitative details were not ineffable, but Han was lazy and disinterested in them, so he contented himself with lists, and these lists became the whole of perceptual experience for him. Is it any wonder that over time, before his time ended, Han began to focus his narratives on dictators who shared his predilection for pared-down environments and people?

Could Han keep going like this? It turned out that he could not. Thinking about the art of writing and doing it as an improvisor would did not open new cycles of vitality for him. He went away, perhaps of his own accord, but either way, writing had not renewed him.

VIII

GHOSTS IN THE Korean imagination are almost always long-haired women wearing white hanboks. Their gnarled hair drips with water, for they are usually the spirits of women who have drowned themselves after having met a personally insurmountable level of injustice. There is a limit for everyone. In the name of revenge, these despairers, while still alive, threaten their tormentors with suicide. After thoroughly terrifying whoever their male (or occasionally female) enemies are, they drown themselves, submerging their bodies in vats, streams, ponds, lakes, or rivers. This final act is evocative of bathing, of returning to the womb. Is that it—suicide can be for self-soothers? Once the dead turn undead, they return to terrorize their foes even more, until their foes lie inert, forced to stare into the faces of those they had abandoned after impregnating, raping, beating, financially exploiting, et cetera. The hairdresser was becoming Kai's own watery ghost, if a somewhat unusual one in that she was spawning other ghosts as she dwindled away herself.

The hairdresser was a mother. She had a four-year-old daughter whom Kai had seen a handful of times—never in any extended sense, only briefly when he picked up or dropped off the hairdresser at the house she shared with her mother. The little that Kai had seen of the hairdresser's homelife surprised him. Pliant as she was before Kai, she was wont to strike her daughter very hard and committedly. On her days off, while her mother sold side dishes at a market that was not nearby, the hairdresser did nothing. On a typical day when the hairdresser was not at the salon, she would rest on the ground, covered by a duvet before her television set. Her body would be curled in the shape of a skinny moon as she looked at whatever it was she was looking at, attempting to relax, forget salon business. She would sleep until her eyes opened naturally, play games on her phone for the next one to two hours, and eat snacks, usually shrimp-flavored chips, dried squid, dried mango, raw ramen straight out of the bag, or chocolate-filled wheat crackers modeled after baseballs. As she chewed on her finger food, she would watch eating channels in which civilians not unlike herself ate for the camera. (The hairdresser was indifferent to cooking channels.) These eaters either ate small quantities of something special or large ones of something cheap for the pleasure of their viewership.

One day, the hairdresser was watching a thin man in his early twenties consume twenty servings of fried chicken and kimchi rice with baked corn on the side. All the while he commented on the food's texture, how enticing the wings were, his new pants, his new nose that he had bought with his television money, and how he was taking more bathroom breaks than usual this session. The hairdresser's mouth was not watering, and yet something was rumbling. He was a precious eater, slurping and crunching a bit louder than was appropriate for a meal, but that was probably for her benefit over the airwaves. She was not, however, privy to the contents of his mouth. He did not go that far even as he opened his mouth quite wide, displaying all his teeth before biting into anything. The hairdresser was curious about what else went into his mouth, whether he only ate in the room that he taped himself in, whether he duped his viewers by vomiting in between takes, and whether eating was the only activity of his that he taped.

The eater's throat was thickening. It was a wonder that he was not choking. Watching that man eat in the prime of his life was infuriating. With his oversized jaw and mouthful of teeth, chuckling, burping his way through fast-food meals she could only vicariously experience, he dared to make such easy money by eating what one should not be eating. It is a shame that humans are so stubbornly myopic. They are such visual, dim-witted pillars, lacking in even hindsight, trapped in their own immanence. Despite knowing how to escape from pain (or gravitate toward it, if one prefers), few do. If one wants material luxuries, one requires an education or apprenticeship. If a formal education is unappealing, the domain of show business awaits. (Art proper remains too unpredictable.) For the entertainment industry, one also needs to attend classes to groom one's talent and not be discouraged by the prospect of bartering one's body along the way. To have any glamour job often necessitates a self-assurance derived from desperation, plenitude, or both. The gall of someone with nothing left to lose, a preternatural attractiveness that is buttressed by the right temperament, the cushion of a nice family, or all the above can help open doors. Everyone knows these truisms about working. Yet few have the discipline to do anything. They see the door but refrain from picking up the key to unlock it. The decent-minded feel some contempt for themselves for failing to do the obvious. Everyone knows what to do to live like those they admire, but few do what it takes if the path feels inconvenient. They prefer to tape themselves eating.

The hairdresser stirred, then went still, stiffening. The pitter-patter of feet could be felt through the floor. It was her daughter coming in from another room. It must have been morning, sometime before nine. The hairdresser had not checked her phone yet, having only been thinking about what she felt like ingesting.

The child was now standing next to her, touching her shoulder tentatively, now kneeling for a caress, a cuddle. She was such a lovable thing, so desperately wanting to be cosseted. Her hair was clean, smelling like nothing. She was not deaf like her.

Mommy, the child was mouthing at her. *Mommy, are you awakey, wakey?* The hairdresser was half-upright but lay down again, pulling the child close to her, spooning her. The child hummed with contentment. She could not have been happier. Her mother was stroking her hair now, brushing her fingers through it, patting her forehead every now and then as both observed the skinny one on screen consuming an entire chicken farm by himself. A few minutes in, the child turned toward her—something was coming. The hairdresser knew the child wanted a particular something, had tiptoed in for a reason.

Are we going to school today? I am ready. I am all dressed. I ate what Grandmommy left for me. I brushed my teeth, washed my face, am dressed. Mommy, I am ready. The child always spoke very slowly so that her mother could follow her mouth moving. But she already sensed the answer by the languid way her mother continued caressing and patting her. If her mother was going to take her to school, she would have gasped, jumped up, and started bustling around since her daughter was running direly late to school that day. But her mother was resting easy at that moment, her gaze never straying from the screen.

The mother's indifference would be remembered by the child. That morning would not last as a separate memory but fade into a larger cloud of feeling that dampened the daughter's interactions with her friends and lovers, an unattractive fatalism that tainted every word in passing, that made her strive less hard to get anything because she knew there was no point in trying. The trying was tiring, a gratuitous trial. No one would strain for her. No one would go out of their way for her.

The hairdresser, still watching the chicken killer, said, *I do not know about today. Are you sure today is the day? Next time, next time—Mommy is feeling a bit tired after a long week. I promise to make it better, to take you tomorrow.* She snuggled in closer, drawing the child in ever closer while modulating her voice, rendering it more pitiful. The mother's instinct to radiate goodwill by firming her body had the expected effect of softening the child's own. The questioning was over. Both would gurgle in their sleep over the next few hours. They were shallow breathers, their chests rising and falling quickly.

Half a day passed, and in the late afternoon, the hairdresser's mother came home. Her daughter and granddaughter were still on the floor. That did not mean they had been there this whole time, did it? *Hello, hello there, little ones, hello. Why do I not see your backpack out, my cute thing? Why are you just lying there?* The grandmother could feel something prickling. Something was not right. It was not terribly wrong just yet, just not right. Everyone's poses were too limp and listless. The pair on the floor seemed too embedded in the ground, as though they had never left it (although they had earlier in order to go to the bathroom and forage for food, that sort of thing). And the curtains were drawn, which was strange. Why keep the room dim when there was more than enough light outside?

The mother caught her grown daughter's eyes, searching. *Did you take the child to school today?*

The hairdresser sighed and huddled closer to the television.

Did she go to school today? the elder asked, louder and slower.

A sigh followed: *We were both tired. It could not be helped. She can rest one day. It is not the worst thing for her. Children should be able to rest easy from time to time.*

The grandmother, who was in her forties, tensed. She was angry. *This is the second day in a row that the child has missed preschool. Do you want to sink her? She needs to go to school. Do you not care? She is your own blood-daughter. And can you not see how she wants to go and learn and play with her friends?*

The elder was speaking more briskly than usual, and louder, while nudging her daughter's upper back with her foot, digging her toes in at certain intervals for emphasis. The child was paying no attention, placidly watching television while all this was going on. The grandmother kept berating and nudging her daughter with her foot, speaking louder and louder, her face twisting from the fatigue of it all. The hairdresser amiably ignored her. She ignored her until a tremor ran through her when she realized she was in the mood to go out for a smoke. But there was no cigarette money on her. She needed cash for cigarettes. It was time for this mother to face the big mother.

As her mother kept using her foot like a cane to prod her, the hairdresser sat up and turned around, making the motion for smoking. Her mother understood her in an instant. *No, no, I do not have any cigarettes. No money either, no cash today, do not even try me. Do not think about it. No, no, go away.* The grandmother retreated and took up the task of sorting laundry on the other side

of the bedroom that also served as a dining room. The hairdresser
stood up and plodded up to her, rubbing her hands together,
entreating. Thus began their ritual where the eldest mother would
flit back and forth, trying to avoid her grown daughter while
keeping her hands busy with some domestic chore. That day, the
hairdresser predictably followed her, trying to grab her wrists.

I need it. I need something. The hairdresser spun around and
headed toward the child, taking those few steps with great force
and urgency. The grandmother grew alarmed, following her
daughter with her eyes. The younger woman knelt beside the
child, who now started paying attention to what was going on
around her. The child looked up, turning away from the television
set upon sensing some physical commotion beside her. *Give me
money for a pack*, the hairdresser repeated to her mother. As her
mother watched her without saying anything, she lurched down,
pulled the child up by her hair, and started smacking her in the
face as one would hit an adult behind an office's closed doors.
The slaps rang out. The child burst out screaming. The grandmother rushed across the room and threw herself down, trying to
shove her body in between her daughter's and granddaughter's,
using all her might to disentangle the hairdresser's fingers from
the little one's hair. Those fingers, however, clenched harder with
every tug, their nails clawing into the child's scalp.

It took less than a minute for the eldest to quit. She patted the
hairdresser's upper arms, backing away to gesture that she was
getting the money; there was no need to keep beating the child.
As the hairdresser's mother turned around to get some cash out of
her wallet, which was hidden in a fanny pack placed underneath
her turtleneck, the hairdresser gave the child a few more lashes

across the face. *This one really does look too much like her father.*
She let go after the last thunks landed. The child bleated pite-
ously, wiping her tears when she could, her howls subsiding into
sobs that she muffled with her hands when she saw her mother
turning toward her once more. Her mother could be very irritated
by the sight of her chest heaving and her mouth growing wider if
she was sobbing loudly. That kind of display would provoke
more strikes. The key was to not make any sudden moves, to not
shrink back too quickly, but to lie still and cry discreetly, letting
her grandmother take care of things, get her mother out of
the house.

The cash having been exchanged, the environment eased at
once. The hairdresser had gone.

When Kai was once walking up to the house where the hairdresser lived with her mother and daughter, he heard much
shrieking, the same noise that the hairdresser's neighbors heard
all the time. That sound whirled around Kai as he went in without
knocking. The hairdresser's daughter ran up toward him, tugging
at his sleeve, begging him to help her. The hairdresser was following her but came to a standstill upon sighting Kai. The grandmother, who was gripping her daughter's arm, likewise stilled
upon seeing this guest at their door, an unfamiliar cylinder who
was patting the child who was walling herself off behind him, hun-
kering down behind his legs, squirming to have Kai shield her.
The grandmother came forward, picked up the bramble, bowed to
Kai, and told him that they had been readying to leave the house,
so please enjoy spending time with her daughter. It was nice for
friends like Kai to visit, pay their respects. Kai nodded back, patting
down the child's hair as the squirmer herself burrowed her head

deeper into her grandmother's neck, hiccuping from her inner tension weakening.

Kai stooped down to take off his shoes without idling to give the hairdresser's family a reason to make their escape more swiftly without having to exchange any more forced pleasantries. He took the hairdresser's elbow, ushering her deeper into her own house as though she were the guest. He sat himself down, gesturing for coffee. He made a conscious effort to not look at the woman strangely. She was grateful for his outward apathy and scurried around to do his bidding, warming up water on the stove, rustling around the cupboards for a packet of instant something. As she hastened around, her feet pushed aside whatever was cluttering the floor, pushing things beneath other things or toward the walls, not abandoning them in the room's center.

This was when she wanted Kai the most. When her gratefulness was less inflected with resentment, it shimmered into a sensation akin to a rueful yearning, a closed mouth that was watering. *Kai is appealing because he does not care about people staring at me sometimes. Kai, that self-assured piece, is not embarrassed in the least. He is comfortingly predictable, cycling through stages of reflection and repentance, with everything fading away by the end when he returns to his baseline. That is his charm, who he is. That comforts me. Kai is uninterested in change or in changing me; that is comforting. That means I can always count on him for money, unlike some other purses. And Kai knows that I do not like the name my mother gave me, so he tosses out endearing names for me when we are in bed or out on dates, pinching my nose as he says them while mostly not looking at me but at his phone. And look at how he comes to see me and save me from embarrassment on this day of all days, how he keeps me company and feeds my family.*

The hairdresser was thinking and moving around and making coffee, aware that Kai was taking off his jacket behind her, settling onto the ground in a cross-legged position. When she set the coffee down on the low table, he motioned for her to go wash up. Kai liked his company clean, smelling either like nothing or artificial forests. She needed to lather and shave her underarms as well. Leaving her genitals unshaved was fine. Kai would sip on his coffee slowly without grimacing or turning on the television for distraction as she showered for him.

Before Kai would tape her later that night; before they got to the business of his holding his phone this way and that, resting it against the television at last so as to capture all of her without showing his face; before he would catch her pretending to sniffle as she wound her body to look better for the recording eye; before his tongue strained toward her miniature pencil; before he would get his fill of those close-ups of her genitals dripping with a paste that had the consistency of melted butter; before he would spread her into an earthbound eagle and push into her rear as she alternately contracted her slit and puffed it outward; before he could stick four fingers into her cunt and shake them for salt water; before such rituals, Kai wanted her to have something from him. Kai told her, *Why not take this opportunity to write out how I make you feel, the desires I leave unfulfilled? How about that? How about you write out what you wanted but never received from me? What do you say?*

She was flabbergasted. Was this some new game, a trick to get her to further compromise herself before him, invite jeers for saying something sincere when Kai only wanted to play? He assured her that the request was made in good faith, to go ahead, do it. And hurry since there was much to get through before her mother and daughter returned that day.

The hairdresser began scribbling. She started the exercise in a tentative, self-mocking way, but the mood distilled into something purer as the moment deepened. It grew serious in not a bad way. One of the notes that she wrote on a piece of newspaper went something like: *You are too proud. You need to know how the soil feels when your knees are fixed to it.*

Kai wrote back, *What is it that you like to say? One's eyes have to be happy for the spirit to be happy. Are your eyes happy now?*

The hairdresser, not with her pen but with her eyes, was signaling, *Still too proud, Kai. Who told you that you could look at me? Lower your eyes this instant. You want others to be lewd, yet you can be so unerotic many a moment. Are you a god to be above the rules like this?*

Kai looked up at the ceiling, asking her, *Would you like me to die?*

She nodded, showing a grimacing expression that was actually a way of smiling. *Yes, I think so. I myself want to live, though.*

There were more notes passed back and forth between the pair (less frank versions, to be fair, as the messages shown here have been embellished to include what the two were thinking as they wrote). All the things people say about wanting more desperately to live once they encounter disease and death—those feelings were pooling inside the hairdresser in dense puddles that day.

The day she and Kai wrote these notes back and forth was one of their last days together. For she did not see Kai much that winter. And that night, after Kai had left with the footage he wanted, the hairdresser beat the child even harder for having run to Kai for shelter. She kicked the child's stomach, and as the child doubled over on the floor, she jabbed her heel into the small of the child's back before turning her over to hit the bridge of her nose with an open palm. How dare she run to Kai? *Mother, get out of the way. Just see what happens if you try to stop me.*

IX

KAI WAS GOING to see Jung. He was going to visit Jung at her office. Jung was engaged in a cold war every so often with yet another friend who put on airs of being noble when she was merely being unpleasant. Or maybe Jung was the oversensitive one, but how could Kai say this? How could he say to her what he really thought about her: that Jung liked so few of her friends at any given moment that it frequently made him tired and nervous?

This time, Kai had called Jung to arrange a meeting because he had caught wind that Jung was having problems finalizing her engagement to someone he had never met. The person she was seeing had a younger sister and a mother who were united against her in an insidious way. Their hostility was infiltrating every part of Jung's relationship. Together, the potential mother-in-law and sister-in-law made small talk in front of the man with whom Jung held an understanding. They would ask him certain questions, probing him gently in a way that made Jung discreetly the fool, an avaricious one out of touch with reality. Even though Jung always sat on her knees in their presence, took the oily foam off a stew's surface before serving them bowls of that same stew for dinner, and observed the majority of traditional observances in a neutral way (not because she was a woman and this was expected of her, but because she was younger, nicer, and better bred)—even though she did all of these things—she was being denigrated by his family because she had serious conversations with him about how much he was earning in relation to how much he could given his educational background. Jung was being painted like a painted woman who would not be satisfied with anything. She made her lover uneasy and resentful, so he allowed his family to stack their cards against her. And now it looked as though there would be trouble finalizing the engagement. It might never go through at all. Jung needed comfort. So Kai came to see her.

Waiting for Kai in the lobby before her company's security guards, Jung, like the hairdresser, wondered whether Kai felt lonely. Was that the price one paid for ignoring the rules? From Jung's perspective, Kai was treating people indifferently, some-times disrespectfully on purpose, getting involved with those who could never gain his family's blessings. Kai had even begun supporting a host these days, Jung had heard through mutual friends recently, someone he had met when the latter was still in middle school. If Kai kept this up, he would never get married. That nose would be turned upward forever, wrinkling with a patrician disdain for both the working and upper classes, a dis-dain that could potentially curdle into a boring, everyday kind of misanthropy.

Jung chuckled in her head thinking about how Kai always thought people were trying to make passes at him when no one was looking sometimes. Not all the time, of course, since Kai was not delusional (sometimes people were, in actuality, looking at him), but enough here and there to make him seem a bit sad. Kai was too proud and inflexible, idealizing the Japanese too much, imagining that he was a part of their kindred circle while revil-ing them for their arrogance. When Jung was annoyed with Kai for whatever it was before they reconciled, she enjoyed reminding herself that Kai was not as attractive as he thought he was, although Kai was, to be fair, quite attractive. But Jung was annoyed with how Kai was spending less and less time with his friends, even Jung herself, as he settled into his self-anointed role as a regular Timon of Athens. Seoul was hardly Athenian, and that was not necessarily a bad thing.

It was Kai's duty to be present whenever Jung wanted him to be present. What else was he good for? He did not work that hard for a living. He was not as drained by work as everyone else around him was. He made decent wages. Kai had no excuse for making himself scarce like this—how trifling. Jung was too rankled by Kai's comfortable circumstances to pay much heed to a story he liked to enshroud his life with lately, a narrative regarding some vague hurt inflicted by one of his former lovers that had descended too deep, the physical symptoms of grief having allegedly recircuited something inside, numbing things without end—how terrible for Kai.

In Jung's mind, this breakup was a story that had happened long ago. No one cared anymore, and even if they did still care, everyone was preoccupied with their own living. Everyone grows tired of such slumps, and then their tiredness grates on others who have their own enervations to be rid of. No one possesses the stamina to care about another's troubles in an extended fashion. Even news of the terminal illnesses of others earn a limited amount of attention before the business of living intrudes upon everyone, swerving all back to their own interests and daily activities. Everyone is selfish, everyone is tired, everyone is trying to stay busy. This is not out of spite or some deeper malice. It is just that living is hard, and time keeps moving without stopping. That is the brutishness of it. *Give me indefatigability or give me nothing.*

It was precious how Kai signaled in his trademark way how bitter he felt to be condemned to live like this interminably. He would indicate these feelings in a bid to provoke a question or two, a kind word from Jung, but Jung was feeling cranky these days. Kai was not as worldly and hardened as he made himself out to be. Kai was, in truth, quite decent and purehearted in his own way. One look at his parents could convince the casual observer that their clean wells of spiritual vitality must have passed something along to Kai. It was not moral vitiation that would get Kai but inertia maybe. He was so accustomed to winning that when he lost, it was a sight to see.

Jung stopped reflecting on the matter, catching herself letting Kai win again, gain the upper hand. How did he do it? Jung had enough serious troubles of her own these days. She certainly could not spare any energy to linger over things that had happened a lifetime ago to Kai. Jung needed to concentrate her energies on preventing her marriage negotiations from crumbling.

If she indulged in a stray thought during these anxious times, it was whether she would keep indulging Kai after she married. Would she and Kai keep stealing away together from time to time? Or would she stay happily married in the modern sense, remaining monogamous, finding solace in her children, keeping passionately abreast of work, and thinking fewer cynical thoughts about what kind of human being she wanted to be as a totality before the end that was coming?

Now Jung felt more kindly disposed toward Kai. He had recently, in one of his drunken moments, confessed to her that he liked to think that he would have married her had fate not ruined him, getting pitifully and damnably in the way. Jung had laughed and poured Kai another drink, saying that he was too sensitive for her to have ever considered him a viable long-term candidate. (Privately, Jung told herself that Kai could not be relied upon, especially after that blow to his self-esteem from that one, his great love, whom he had thought had been so delectable but could have been entirely something else.) Kai had then sighed, *Are you saying this to get back at me for our first time?* to which Jung replied, *You are pretty when you try to run deep; it becomes you.* Kai told her to hush afterward, to not be so biting toward him; it was not nice; he did not like it when she was like that; she needed to be nicer to him always; she was not being charming. It was a shame: Kai had once been promising for Jung. And now he was a bit sad to look at.

But there Kai was, walking toward her in her office building's lobby. He looked the same as he had during that conversation when he had brought up the subject of marriage—maybe a little more slumped over and sleepy-seeming, a bit bloated, with a few more barely discernible but still-present fine wrinkles under his eyes, his hair thinning. His breath could be better. Kai looked at her, winking. He asked her directly, *Are you feeling cynical today? What happened, ugly?*

It was a fine day for a lunch date. The two decided to go eat cold buckwheat noodles. *How is work?* Kai asked while they were in the middle of settling into their seats, before they submitted their orders and began the wait for their dishes to come out. The eatery was small and cozy, one of those family-run establishments located down a side road near Jung's office. It was a famous one, which accounted for the din at that hour, for how the place teemed with bodies, and for the inward gaze of its servers who were working well and briskly.

I have an hour at the moment, so that is nice. But the day is tedious to be honest.

Oh, how so?

Kai was fond of hearing Jung go at it. She made a higher art of it, the way she ripped into things, tore centers apart. She had a very tasty way of cursing and attacking, very virile, alive, immediate, and heartwarming. She emanated a great humanness, sparing the heart of nothing, not even herself, when she went at it. Naturally, she was more generous with herself. Who was not? She was nicer to listen to than men because the men in Kai's vicinity had an ostentatious air about them. These machos overperformed their cursing, making Kai wish he were eavesdropping upon the women who worked at the markets, heating the air up as they did with their slurs when they were feeling stingy. The way that Jung did it was best, though. She never did it as a substitute for boasting. She only addressed what was in her power, trying to be as objective as possible. She had high standards, and she met most of them herself on a daily basis. She was lustily bloodless, quite the butcher.

Jung could see Kai smiling at her, looking down at the table from time to time to savor what she was saying as she was saying it. She felt splendid. Kai was openly admiring her. He knew how to inspirit her, winning himself back into her good graces by the way he appreciated her brittler flavors.

So did you win the account? Did you get the money?

You bet I did, Jung clarified. *Oh yes, I did, did I do that. I showed them. I handled it.* Jung never held back from telling Kai the technical details surrounding such delicate transactions and power plays at her office because that was the greatest emblem of their friendship, the way they both showed their mutual caring. Kai would tell Jung everything, including the pettiest trifles that fell under his work dealings, and Jung would do the same for Kai, sparing nothing since their intimacy was nourished on this grousing. How many would she break to her will today, crushing with the weight of her force, her energy, that frightening internal coolness? How would she win her cases without going too far in her battles and irretrievably hurting feelings? With each character, Jung had to read their personality profile and treat that person in a way that kept her in her dominant position. It was all irksome, minus the few moments of excitement when a victory like this week's came in—when Jung won over big clients, closed deals, helped her fellows and superiors save face before difficult customers, or suavely cowed difficult clients into submission. Such triumphs hardened Jung's will to keep fighting at work, keep fighting the good fight without aiming below the belt. They fed her enough so that she would not walk out of her office after saying what cannot be retracted afterward.

It is in the details that affections are formed; broad strokes are reserved for polite conversations with acquaintances. The fewer details one provides, the less of an opening for criticism one invites. The less one shares, the less one deigns to expose oneself. One is putting up one's guard, performing the bare minimum of social etiquette in that case. But a conversation regarding an office slight or sexual rejection can run for over two hours if the speakers are compatible, truly interested in each other. This lunch was Jung's, and Kai had arrived to make Jung feel better, lift her mood as she was feeling down and out of sorts from bickering with her lover's mother and sister. Kai's presence was comforting. And he refrained from touching her, only imparting an embrace when they had met in her office's lobby, a caress on the cheek when she was complaining about someone during lunch, and another embrace and kiss on the cheek when he dropped her off later at her office. But other than these measured gestures, there was no more of that playful cloud that used to hang between them. Kai understood what Jung wanted, how she wanted to keep things now. He understood her. But, Jung wondered, would she ever want him to go back to how he had been with her? Would she ever want Kai to touch her again?

Lives are spent around meals and bedrooms and workplaces, not accounting for the time it takes to float from one scene to the next. That is the brunt of it. Is there anything else? Very little. In these comings and goings, Jung and Kai were speaking and listening to each other—and understanding what was unsaid in between. Kai could feel Jung's prodding him to let certain things go, her impatiently telling him without telling him directly that people like themselves cannot complain too much due to their material comforts. *What about the rest of the world that lies shorn and starving, sharing fatal blows over what is left after locusts have had their share of our fertile lands?* Kai could feel Jung trivializing what he felt, that his story of himself was boring and self-indulgent to her.

Kai said back to her without speaking, *Jung, do not do that. Do not dismiss this. If you act like that, no one can mourn. Everything will turn to an unseemly wallowing; everyone must suffocate in their muted gnashings. What are we supposed to do then, just lie on our sides, shallow breathing until we flop over dead, having uttered not one word about our disappointments? Do not be like this, Jung. You do not even believe it yourself and would want more under-standing. Do not be insincere: hard on others, soft on yourself; weak before the strong, strong before the weak. You are better than that. A sea of ships keeps turning to ashes in my mouth. How do I stop that—this aftertaste?*

Jung could sense something of his thoughts, Kai thought. She noticed him looking at her, stiffening, his smile thinning, his voice assuming a formal quality, quieting at unexpected times during their chatting. She could tell when Kai wanted to teach her a lesson about something that she was doing, but he never did it passive-aggressively by complaining about that same quality in another person (like someone else Jung knew and did not like). He just became formal and quiet.

Jung picked up the tab and signaled to Kai that she wanted him to walk her back to her office building. Kai obliged in his way. He said deliciously vicious things about her co-workers, par-ticularly about one whose eyebrows were placed too far apart on her forehead. *There was a frog from my secondary school who had looked like that,* Kai said. Kai would fall in with Jung's moods, let-ting her steam and bubble up. Kai liked it, and Jung liked Kai for liking it.

After waving Kai along while telling him to stop eating badly, Jung sighed and pushed her floor's elevator button. It was tiring to socialize at lunch. It was nice and energizing in the moment, but still. It was more energy expended, more walking, more

gesturing, more having to be amusing and sympathetic, more
wanting to be seductive without crossing over into that final
moment, more money on trinkets wasted. But then if she did not
relieve herself on lunch dates like this, she felt that she would
explode in her office. Sitting for too long in a chair without feeling some fresh air on her face was becoming unbearable, yet taking breaks with someone else took more than a little something
out of her; and yet taking breaks efficiently alone was also boring.
This is the human condition. All choices do not bring about an
ultimate fullness. But one makes do regardless.

The lunch meal between Jung and Kai was followed by
another meal less than three months later with their usual friend
group and a few new faces mixed in. Min could not make it, but
there was Jung, Han (still very much alive at the time, no one
having any inkling that he was in the process of developing an
expensive drug habit), Kai, Yoon, and Yoon's new girlfriend. Yoon
now had a girlfriend after having gotten unofficially divorced. He
and his wife were living in separate homes, but their separation
had not been finalized on paper since she was as yet uncon-
vinced that she had everything she needed from him for her self-
maintenance. His new companion was on the younger side
without being as young as he had gone before when he had liked
them younger.

Jung's fiancé would join the group shortly. He did not like the
idea of Jung mingling within a mixed-gender group without his
presence. It was not that he did not trust her (although that was a
smart instinct) but that he did not consider it befitting. He was cut
from the old cloth, and that was a part of his charm for Jung so
long as he did not push it. This was the same person whose mother

and sister were atrocious to Jung. Still, he was an even-keeled one in that he had agreed to go along with Jung when she let him know that she was getting an abortion. It was his, but Jung was not interested in a hastily arranged wedding ceremony and not in the mood to spend all her savings on child-rearing just then, so their planned marriage would go ahead without an infant.

The night was not rejuvenating. Nothing, not the appearance of her fiancé, made Jung feel any different. Yoon's date kept prattling on. Yoon himself did not seem sheepish about her. He seemed indifferent or somewhat desirous of attention at best given how he continued caressing her knees, squeezing her waist while looking about distractedly. Kai looked bored and the same amount of bloated as he had been weeks before. Han was politely engaged with everyone at the table, doing all the heavy lifting tonight. *Bless him for trying to make conversation with Yoon's extra, for dusting the table with general topics. The food here is average. The waiters are merely proficient. The lights are too bright, and my fiancé is making that face that promises we are going to have an unpleasant chat later. Is this all there is?* Jung puzzled.

Two days after this dinner party, Jung experienced what she suspected was a stroke. The left side of her face was blurring, slushing into a shuddering mass. She was sitting in front of her dual-screen desktop in her office's fashionably arranged open floor plan. (Hers was one of the more spacious cubicles located nearest to the windows because of her high position.) Something was not right. Her facial muscles were alternately tingling and burning. Was this what Westerners called a panic attack? Jung had thought until now that this phenomenon was merely a cry for attention rather than a clinical condition, an appetite for receiving caresses while others flurry about with paper bags and say in sotto voce for one to lie down. Did she need a paper bag to exhale into? Her chest was shrinking. A pressure from the distance was wading nearer, thrusting itself up her esophagus to become a sludgy heartburning feeling, one that complemented her facial tingling. The tingling, at any rate, was now turning into paralysis. Jung's words to herself were slurring as her tongue grew heavy in her mouth, a piece of flotsam. She was a fish flopping on an unclaimed deck. What was happening?

Jung did not stop working. She kneaded her own shoulders, exhaling slowly; massaging her hands and feet; pushing their pressure points; and rubbing her cheeks and jowls, each portion of her face that was hurting. Studiously bent over her desk, trying not to draw attention to herself, she pretended to work despite being unable to trek any further. It was fortunate that there were no more meetings that day, no more reasons to interact with anyone.

She did leave early, however, to go straight to the hospital without telling anyone, including her betrothed. *It was nothing*, she told herself, *not a stroke, not anything*. Jung was declared fine at the hospital, checking out in good health a little after dinnertime.

But the matter of why this phantom stroke had happened was left on the table. It was an ominous inquiry for Jung. *Are you unhappy?* the doctor had asked.

Am I unhappy or overly anxious enough to have imagined everything? Jung repeated to herself. *Am I unhappy? Is there ever a time when we are perfectly happy? What does that even mean? I am well enough. He is there. The wedding is coming up without my having to disagreeably intervene in anything. His sister and mother have retreated. Work is working. The years are passing. Life keeps going.* Jung transmitted these thoughts to her doctor—that nothing was out of sorts. There was no vapor inside that was destabilizing her center of gravity. The only thing, if it counted as anything at all, was the question of whether this was it. That was something that Jung asked herself in her spare moments.

The doctor nodded. *I see now. I had the same questions at your age. This is it, you know that already, but it does not have to feel like such a bleak answer.* The doctor leaned toward Jung over the table, advising her to work less intensely. Not fewer hours overall—the doctor was not advocating shirking. She meant for Jung to stop pushing herself so hard mentally while at work, to try to be present without over-heating the kiln past what it was capable of enduring. And to treat herself by doing fun things more frequently. And to speak with her fiancé, to share these feelings. When Jung told the doctor that their relationship was not like that, that that was not their style of emotional intimacy, the doctor nodded again, understanding at once what Jung meant without her having to elaborate.

The engagement ended shortly afterward. It was obvious that Jung was acting without reflecting on anything, moving around because to do nothing was unaffordable and dreary. Still, what used to suffice no longer did. Jung could not find a reason for anything she was doing. This sense of a fan stilling somewhere within was not about the aborted fetus. The government insists that an abortion would plague a woman with guilt until she drives her automobile into the Han River, but matters are only a big deal when one is taught to treat them that way. Jung was not that upset about having scraped out that cellular bundle. Her episode was about what, then? If not from regret over the infant that might have been had she been more invested or romantic anguish from having made unwise plans with someone who it was awkward to make conversation with, then from where had her stroke-that-was-not-a-stroke originated?

Jung's appetite for food remained unaffected. She did not feel like quitting work and moving elsewhere, spending money on younger dates, or having older dates spend their accounts on her. Family was nearby without being welcoming. *What is the matter,* Jung asked herself, *when no one is dying of cancer?* She was not as stricken as Kai was by flashbacks while walking. (Wisps of his most beloved former lover whining, *I am tired,* kept intruding into Kai's peripheral vision, which is to say that Kai kept having flashbacks of when he would doze off and awake to find that person curled around him.) Jung called Kai.

He came to her after picking up the call. Not right away but a few days later. Jung told Kai, *I want to go somewhere.* This was what she truly wanted. *All right,* Kai replied, *all right.* So they went ice-skating. Jung appreciated Kai's unexpected choice. *This should be fun.* Fun was much welcome at this point in the late summer. *How could this past winter have lasted for so long?* Jung pondered. The cold had gone on. This new monsoon season felt nicer. Each one had been more humid and heated than its predecessor. It was a treat to visit a place that was an homage to the spirit of winter.

The challenge was to keep one's balance, not fall over and have one's fingers sliced into a sushi salad. The rink was cold, the activity pleasantly fast-paced. Kai had correctly read her. Jung thought at one point, *I want to be left alone on the ice*—and Kai left her alone, skating ahead or behind or to the side. They skated separately before coming back together, then separating again in cycles. They hurled through the air, becoming the air's very own crystals. Jung was skilled enough to brake cleanly. It was pleasant to see ice flakes flare up and settle back down when she sprayed Kai's ankles with them after braking near him to tease him. Jung did not hum as she skated, although every so often she had the urge to. She was not looking for that kind of attention. It was too bad that the rink did not turn on any music that she could lose herself in, something rhythmic and melodically rebounding, circling, ever circling. Jung believed that the rink's operators were intimidated by the thought of their skaters possibly becoming distracted by such music and falling. Or were the employees just idle? Jung did not have any earphones to wear at that moment, and she was too lazy to get off the ice and go fish them out of her purse that was locked away. That was too much. She was still entitled to be wistful about her absent earphones, however. That she could do.

Kai motioned that he was getting off the ice to take a break. He signaled for her to keep going. *No, no*, she gesticulated back. *I will take a breather with you. Let us take one together. I do not want to be a lone squid swimming here.* They sat down, commenting about the rink's lack of music. How nice this smidgen of exercise felt. How long it had been since either one of them had gone skating. How strange it was that such activities tended to be dropped from the orbit of most adult lives.

As was their custom, Jung and Kai brooded over certain subjects without sharing them aloud. On Jung's end: *I am very tired, Kai.*

Kai, then, to Jung: *Do not prostrate yourself like this, Jung. It is too early for such staleness. Our batteries have years left to go. Even our elders remain ruddy.*

Such thoughts were in the air, thrumming but unsaid, which was better for the occasion. Kai went to the bathroom and returned. Jung went afterward, each looking after the other's belongings when left alone in charge. They went back out on the ice and skated some more without touching palms. They took another break to smoke outside for a quarter of an hour before returning to continue skating. It was marvelous how they skated for two and a half hours, skating and skating with breaks snuck in to ward off boredom and injuries. Feeling refreshed from the cold air and physical exertion, they had a light, tasteless dinner, something fibrous without too many sauces and spices to enliven it. They drank plenty of water before stopping by Jung's apartment, where both showered, one after another, before lotioning and dressing themselves and styling their hair in separate rooms. At around eight in the evening, they walked to a nearby cinema to watch two films back-to-back. That day was like a day from Jung's and Kai's school days. It was like a playdate from those earlier years.

They might as well have gone window-shopping or to a karaoke room that same night, but both declined. They had gone ice-skating, then to the movies; then they said good night. At the theater, they had watched the closing credits to ensure that nothing was missed. Jung spryly walked herself home, feeling full inside. Kai hailed himself a cab since the subways had closed.

It was a day unlike the others that they had spent together in Seoul. It was as though they were back in school together even though they had never been schoolmates, having only been introduced many years afterward through Yoon. What they did that day was a sweet way of playing. It was not an antidote or permanent alternative to their regular playing around in Seoul's puddles but a sweet supplement to enrich their regular diet. Jung felt energized after a day such as that. So did Kai.

The day after the next (a Monday since Jung and Kai had met on a Saturday) when Jung went back to her office, she did not perform strikingly better. She was not more sanguine or over-bearingly concerned with her cubicle-mates—nothing so flagrant of a shift. She was normal. She worked as usual. But there were no strokes that day and increasingly fewer afterward. There were grueling days, days of rushed paperwork and curses uttered, but the sensation of being human sand falling in reverse gradually dissipated.

Jung did not meet Kai all the time to do such soothing activities. She met others. She rounded out her schedule with an assortment of acquaintances. But she and Kai made sure to go on an outing at least once every other month, trying something new together or something old that they had not experienced in a while. They laughed in each other's presence during these outings and elbowed each other as children do. They enjoyed themselves—lilies in their prime season.

X

IT WAS NOW the winter after the winter that Kai had tried to summit Mount Jiri. It was the winter following that late summer of enjoyably dispassionate skating. It was another winter among winters that were becoming warmer and shorter as the oceans were rising.

Where was Kai to spend the holidays now that his parents were living in separation? Like them, Kai was practical. All three agreed to meet at Kai's father's home. After this Christmas soirée, Kai would remain with his father for a few days before traveling to his mother's apartment. This plan was cobbled together even though none of them had ever rigorously celebrated this European holiday. Hence, there would be no lighted trees, wrapped gifts, carols, candles, baked treats, sweets, or guests in attendance.

Kai had dried out by now after eating only squid and sweet pumpkin potatoes the entire autumn. While he still wept over the phone with his parents fairly frequently, Kai had not wept before them in person in a long time. Tears from a distance were fitting, even charming. Such tears seemed tokens of their collective long-ing to reunite—not the parents with each other but each parent for Kai. Each wanted to live with him and be fussed over in the same way each fussed over him. For all three lived alone: Kai dwelt in Seoul, Kai's father at the Yellow Mountain's base, and Kai's mother in Busan. As Kai packed for the weeklong vacation, he felt that weeping in the presence of others was now embarrassing. Had not the time passed for him to be wailing about anything?

Only the immediate family would be present this Christmas. In the years ahead, too, when these three family members would celebrate the wintry holidays together, there would be no other relatives present, as years had passed since Kai had met any of them. His paternal branch remained a mist. Kai's father never spoke of his own due to a combination of guilt at having been absent from the deathbeds of his parents, his wife's grudge (although her feelings were dimming as their instigators had since been cremated), and his own equivocations toward his kin for filling him with a great many uncomfortable memories. Who knew where Kai's paternal cousins were or what they were doing? The same went for Kai's paternal uncle, who had inherited everything, and aunts. Whether his father had two or three sisters, Kai never knew. He had never bothered asking.

Of his maternal cousins, Kai was aware of a little more. His maternal grandmother detested her younger son because he had sired only daughters, even though his eldest daughter was accomplished enough to have earned a spot at the nation's top university. Her achievement did not surprise Kai. Her father had wed a sensible, industrious type who compensated for not being a classical beauty by having pleasantly rounded features. Kai's eldest maternal uncle had married an individual who had morphed unpleasantly over time through her physician husband's ill-won inheritance money.

Caressing Kai lovingly when he was a child and even now when Kai had become a middle-aged adult, his father had not changed. Or had he? Kai's father's Chungnam apartment now showcased photographs of himself with his male friends. He was placing his own touch everywhere, declaring himself to be his own person. The same person who, while married, had no photographic documentation of his past was evolving into a well-photographed man about town, one who kept up a manageable schedule of tee times, karaoke sessions, drinking parties, and road trips to historical eateries. No one pried into whether this schedule included female company. Kai's father was careful not to say anything.

The apartment was heating up nicely as it was snowing outside the sliding windows in the living room. Kai was still at the Yellow Mountain, having yet to have gone to Busan. Kai's father was preparing his own seafood version of dark gravy noodles, a dish Kai was fond of.

What are you doing, Kai? His father was addressing him from the kitchen, yet he seemed far away.

I am looking out the window, Father.

Thinking about what?

I do not know, maybe about how much it is snowing. It usually does not snow this much these days because of atmospheric warming.

The snow, I see. Yes, I heard certain storms are brewing, as cold and warm currents are meeting somewhere in the middle.

The conversation drifted toward how the food was looking. The gravy and seafood smelled good. Portions would be generous. No one would go hungry. A number of spicier side dishes that Kai's mother would have never allowed for health reasons were displayed on the table. Kai continued to avoid inquiring whether his father missed his ex-wife or the particulars of why their marriage ended. Maybe his father was mostly the same, which was to Kai's advantage, but Kai had not changed for the better, remaining the same egoist who had covered a corner of his father's face in a scrapbook by accident, overlaying it with another image when his father deserved more from him, had saved him from expulsion several times the year that scrapbook had been made.

This is very good, Kai said aloud, looking straightforwardly into his father's eyes.

Those eyes grew friendlier. *Is that so?*

Yes, it is so. You are a good cook.

No, no, it is nothing.

It is something.

All right, I am glad to hear that.

Are you cooking for yourself these days? (*Do you eat your meals alone or with someone else?* was a question that Kai did not risk.)

I eat at work. Work takes care of the majority of my meals. Coming back home to cook for myself feels unnecessary and tiring.

Cooking, eating, and making small talk drew out the pair's delight in each other. These were the matters that lasted, never growing obsolescent. They simply endured. The kitchen warmed as Kai and his father curved toward each other.

The way Kai's mother lived as a single person was not too dissimilar from her former husband's. But while he was mostly content in Chungnam, she very much did not like living in Busan; she would have much preferred to live in Seoul. Being as near as they were to Japan, Busan's inhabitants were even said to resemble the Japanese in their sharp features, although their temperamental differences were marked for Kai's northern-biased family. The Japanese were known to be rule-abiding, publicly even-tempered, and fastidious in their professional and grooming habits; Busan's people had a reputation for being fiery, hard-drinking, lawless, and prone to violent outbursts at the slightest provocation. Its women, Kai's mother believed, were uniquely abrasive. For her, Busan was the peninsula's equivalent of *Sicily*, *the American South*, and *Boston* all in one. It was a city of thugs and boors, with deep historical affiliations with organized crime syndicates. Its dialect was thick and contoured like a beak. With its compendium of trills and elongated vowels, the Busan twang was one of those things that Kai's family quietly hated. Kai's mother stiffened whenever she heard it, which meant that she was strained all the time.

To improve her moods, she visited the same nail salon once a month and was received by the same twenty-something-year-old man. A younger male colleague in his forties also called her twice a day on most days to gossip about nothing. Kai's mother would never become flustered when these calls rang in Kai's presence. She would coolly pick up the call, tilting away from Kai. She would turn her back to him and scoot away a few meters. Kai did not stare at her disapprovingly during these moments. He kept doing whatever it was that he was doing while listening to how she chuckled without kittenishly twisting her body, assuming an alternately maternal and brotherly persona as she shared incisive details about so-and-so with the caller, exuding a subtle some-thing. Only the faintest of antennas could sense any tremors, but Kai felt them. Something was there in her phone calls, shivering without mewing.

Kai's mother never introduced him to anyone she worked with. When she took Kai with her to work whenever he visited during her workweek, she confined him to her office as she went about her day. Kai was instructed to stay put and to never reveal his face to anybody. Kai never minded these conditions. He was indifferent to, and sometimes amused by, the secrecy surrounding his visits. *Uncomfortable* was the word for how his mother felt about leaking her private life or allowing the boundary between the personal and the professional to become porous. If her co-workers could be vipers, why not be safe rather than sorry? Everyone need not know everything, not that seeing Kai's face amounted to much. Just as importantly, Kai's mother had intuited through her own antenna that Kai tended to look too closely for her comfort at certain people she worked with.

Upon welcoming Kai to her studio, Kai's mother told him, *You need to make your own family. Your father and I are not your family. You are our family, but we are not yours. You should have your own in your age group. You have not been crinkled internally or to the eye that badly, I promise. You are still attractive to newcomers. You can organize the dust storm to your advantage. Have some faith in your peers. You say that you do not enjoy so-and-so's company, finding them shortsighted and homely like a fungus sporing more of itself over clay; why, they do not enjoy yours either.*

She was responding to Kai's words from the past and present, from all those moments when he would excessively attack others (like Jung did) and thereby prompt his mother, as was her way, to look at him from the sides of her eyes without turning her head and murmur that her child was very temperamentally cold about everyday human affairs. Where had he learned this from? In these moments, Kai would feel the import of her side glance and want to be gentler and more loving, not just with her but with the world of others that she came from, the others surrounding her of which he, too, was one.

Kai was becoming more and more in charge of her moods when they were together. Both she and her former husband wanted to be cosseted by their own children as they entered this new phase of separation during their late middle age. As children are indulged by their parents and grandparents and older familiars, so Kai's parents wanted the same treatment from their own children.

Kai's mother brought Kai back to the present. In her studio with Kai after he had arrived from his father's, Kai's mother proceeded to tell him of a documentary about a man who became psychologically unstable after his art school failed and his wife, another unsuccessful artist, left him. He began donning diaphanous black turtlenecks and tights with combat boots everywhere he went. Whether he had purchased multiple copies of the same outfit or touted the same unwashed ensemble day after day was unknown. This failed artist and teacher began dancing everywhere in the attempt to boost his self-esteem, to fool himself into believing that he could be anything for anyone. He was jiggling in the streets, and so was his penis through the sheer fabric he favored.

Kai was piqued by this story, asking his mother for more details as she was putting away groceries. He was moving around as well to help her without getting in the way; when Kai's mother moved around at home for Kai, Kai moved to help her as he did for his father. Kai wiped off items before placing them in the refrigerator. Dinner was going to be good that night since Kai's mother doted on him and it was just after Christmas. There was sushi to be unwrapped, cuts of beef, different lettuce varieties, Brazil nuts, dried persimmons, frozen blueberries, noni juice concentrate, garlic cloves, peppers, spiced cabbage, radishes, and cheesecake, a favorite family dessert. It was going to be a feast for two that evening—how lovely, this love of hers that expressed itself in such alive, lively ways. They ate and conversed, eventually settling in to watch a late-night film about a man who had lost his life through a car accident and returned to his wife as a ghost, covered in a sheet like a hokey Halloween costume to stand watch over her as she went about her life without seeing him. He was waiting for something as the world continued changing, even past that moment when a voice from a neighboring home uttered, *I am also waiting for someone, but I do not think they are coming.*

All this talk of waiting was releasing pearls into a gorge. Kai felt the city's seawaters rising. How far do whales sink when life leaves them? Surely not all the way to the bottom if an ocean has an ever-receding floor.

Where was Kai's brother?

It was time to bring this younger one back into the fold.

Part II

Before Kai had departed from the Yellow Mountain to go to Busan to be with his mother, the whole family had fixated on a single thought. It was a larger elephant in the room than Kai's parents' divorce. It was Kai's brother, who had been discharged from the army less than half a year ago. No one spoke of him that winter, although everyone wanted to. The last time his name had come up in conversation was when Kai's father, overwrought by a soap opera scene, stated that he would beat Kai's brother until his rib cage shattered if he ever caught him impregnating someone in secret.

No one could get in touch with him easily. He answered the family's calls once or twice a month when the tenor of their voice messages turned frantic. As much as they cherished Kai, the elders never thought that Kai had been a good influence on his brother. Kai's parents had always felt uneasy when the two siblings would appear at the dinner table together during their elementary school years. Both children would sport reddish marks on their necks, stirring their parents to look at them strangely. The children were not self-conscious about anything, not shying away from making eye contact, going about their meal indifferently. They liked the taste of salt and had gone about finding this flavor innocently, no matter its source, solidifying their communion with each lick and tentative sharing of their gustatory opinions afterward.

In the army, Kai's brother was not known as a hector like some of his peers. He did not have a taste for tormenting the androgynous, who were ill-equipped to handle themselves before their hardened and restless acquaintances. Nor was he one of those who were excessively concerned about the ages of everyone around them. He was uninterested in forcing younger ones to carry out as many chores as possible, duties such as cleaning toilets, fetching snacks, bowing till their faces scraped the earth, sweeping and salting winter walkways, and tidying common areas. He could not care less about stealing their government allowances for gaming. It was common knowledge that very few of the enlisted went searching for new company on their days off. Most opted to while away the hours with their friends, throwing themselves into smoking, drinking, gambling, gaming, or eating junk food, then falling asleep in groups at a hostel or love motel, bloated and content.

What kind of a person was Kai's brother? Was he one of these piglets at a sleepover? By nature, he was a warm, gentle, good-natured, and social individual who attracted others to him because he helped people save face in different situations. He inspired affection through his confidence; through his calm, mineral-like personality that was quick to cool down; and through his penchant for saying things like *Well, it is hard for us to say since we were not there. Please try not to speak badly of my friends (I mean you, Kai).* Adaptive yet stable, his presence was a broth for his friends and Kai, whose little peanut he was.

What Kai's brother saw in the army made him very tired. He had heard a scream coming from the bathroom stalls one night. Accompanied by thumping, the screaming had faltered before resuming in earnest. Kai's brother did not go there to intervene. He glimpsed an undressed body through the swinging doors as others filed past him to watch or stop whatever was happening. The face and upper torso belonging to the figure on the ground were blocked from view while his exposed lower half was flopping around in time to the sounds of slurping and gagging as voices spiraled upward in a space teeming with human lemmings. Piles of toilet paper were everywhere, seemingly showering down like ghostly confetti, obscuring that flapping, fishlike body. Kai's brother saw all this in a moment's glance, then moved away without linger-ing, walking back to his sleeping quarters, lying down on his cot among the other inert forms, and turning away from the lighted entrance.

Kai's brother related the bathroom incident to Kai upon his return but insisted that it was not the reason that he had withdrawn from the family. He was simply busy. It was challenging to reintegrate into society after a two-year break. No fatal mystery existed. *Please refrain from attributing anything profound to this.* Kai nodded and stopped pushing the matter. Their parents never heard anything about it.

The peninsula's military conscription is so often spoken of, the object of such derision and passion and misery, that it is difficult to survey the military world in an impartial light. What can be agreed upon is that the peninsula's soldiers come to know a truth that dancers, athletes, and pilgrims already know: if the mind is troubled, it is not bad to push the body into exhaustion. Drain the swamp, the viper's poison. If one is tired to the point where one can barely stay awake or eat, then one is too tired to agitate over past resentments—memories of how one's self-image was corrupted. Physical exhaustion can be a boon. Less romantic members of the army do as little as they can to get by, conserving their strength in a race to the bottom so as to avoid winning extra assignments. Romantics do not feign incompetence, instead racing to see who can burn out the swiftest. Kai's brother was in between these two types. He did not play the village oaf. He worked while replenishing himself. He did not assume the persona of one of his drill sergeants who always sat down while giving orders. Sitting down and smoking while everyone else stood was this sergeant's favorite pastime. It was his life's calling, a singular pleasure heightened when his troops ran to do his bidding as he yelled himself hoarse. It was impressive that his squadrons looked up to him. How did he win their affection? Maybe he was a quarter Hawaiian.

Open the door. I know you are in there, pretty one. Kai knocked on his brother's door a week or so later. His brother did not live alone. He lived with a former high school classmate whose mother was a restaurant manager and whose father had passed on by his own volition when his son was in middle school. The years after the IMF crisis had not quieted down for all. The roommate was not there.

The door opened. Kai's brother greeted him, leading Kai to a kitchen roiling in clutter. The smell—something tangy, of unwashed flesh, a muskiness laced with cigarette smoke. Kai's brother appeared sedate, with facial acne. He was wearing basketball shorts without a shirt. He kept scratching one ankle behind the other without radiating too much of a manic air.

I was not expecting you, Kai. Why are you here?

Happy New Year to you too. Is it a crime to come see family on a whim? Must we act like strangers? Make reservations weeks in advance? Are we in the upscale restaurant business?

No, I just meant that I might not have been here when you called. It is customary to call ahead to ensure that you can find whomever you are looking for when you get there.

I know what you meant, but I did not because you yourself made it impossible. You do not want to be located, leaving your calls and messages unanswered. What are you doing these days? How are you spending your time, peanut? Or should I say big-boned coconut?

Kai's brother looked away without looking at anything. Where had the little peanut gone who used to rub his head against Kai's shoulder, secure in the knowledge that he was who Kai loved the most? *If not the army, was it me for constantly pushing him?* This thought floated to the forefront of Kai's mind for a moment before deflating. It was too arrogant to presume that Kai had singlehandedly undone this sapling's bloom. So what was it then? In search of an answer, Kai persevered in making conversation with this recalcitrant one. If one keeps pushing and prodding and prying, a little something happens—a groan materializes in the forest.

Hey, hey you, you in there, younger one. Look at me. Tell me what you are thinking, feeling these days. Why are you submerging yourself? Why have you become a solipsist before me, before our family, unto yourself? Talk to me. Look at me. The lonely planet you have constructed cannot last. I will not let it.

Such were the words that were rushing in a spate through Kai that he did not say. Was Kai's brother still stung from when Kai had taunted him, barred him from taking part in Kai's extracurriculars? Kai, this dastardly one. There was no satisfying answer. These siblings were phlegmatic in temper, inheriting a melancholic bile from their mother's father, the diabetic who departed without tasting so many of the ambitions he had desired for a long time. The younger one lit a cigarette and sucked on it without saying much, offering succinct evasions to Kai's ongoing queries.

I told you, I am fine. I am just tired these days. These days will bleed into better ones once I have more life to give; let it be. Do not stir the waters.

Are you feeling down because you are still unemployed?

No, I had an interview last week. It went well. Work will be starting.

Because the job is, you feel, beneath you.

It is well enough; it satisfies me. It is good enough for Mother and Father.

The army—

Enough of the army. I should not have told you about that episode. It has tainted all our subsequent interactions, made you paranoid about me when I have not been irrevocably scarred by it, which is not to say that the event was not outrageous. I felt terrible about doing nothing at the time, being Mister Impotent. I am telling you, however, that that is not the root of my troubles these days. It is not a stray spring poking into my lower back at night.

This is hard to believe when I see the way that you are living now and how you treat your family. How can you accuse me of over-reacting when I feel as though I am underbaking things?

Fair enough, I understand. I am not in a good way at the moment. I know how things look. But it is not the army, I promise you. It is not the army.

Mother and Father cannot breathe these days. You are becoming the cancer of our family. No one can sleep because of you, because of the way you are carrying on now—drifting, distant.

Kai's voice rose in volume as he went on speaking—agitating, yelling, berating at a frenzied pitch for the next half hour as his brother remained wordless. Hearing about his parents had an effect on him, as he loved them as Kai did. Both siblings were not indifferent to parental anguish, less as a result of the peninsula's ingrained familial attitudes and more due to an adult friendship with their elders. Kai kept shouting and cursing while his brother kept listening and smoking without nodding along. Smoke gathered on the ceiling and the nonlinoleum floors.

Kai's brother's phone rang in the middle of Kai's harangue about losing out on living if things kept going the way they were going. He squinted down, then away, back up toward Kai's face. Kai's chin was where his gaze steadied. His furtive glance down transfixed Kai. Kai blurted out, *What is that? Who is calling?*

No one, nobody.

Liar! Liar, liar, pants on fire. Who is it? Tell me, or I am coming over there and breaking your phone. Take my word for it, so help me.

A woman.

Someone with a temper or unsavory connections. Or both or more of these kinds of things—oh, she is hideous!

You are so shallow. Keep going, sure. That is right. Good for you, goodly Kai. You are so smart, my goodness, you know everything. Break my peanuts while you are at it. Both siblings snickered. The gale between them was returning.

It was funny. Love was bothering Kai's brother. What memories there were of the bathroom incident were not the whole of his problems. Kai's brother did not stay missing after that day. Time kept going as it does, and it faded things for better and for worse— everything besides, on Kai's end, that specimen of brotherly love that contains an element of the right kind of friendship. Kai's brother did not return to where he was before he had entered the army, but after that day, he was not obscenely far off from that place. Eventually, he did begin responding to calls, visiting his parents regularly, calling them to say hello of his own accord, and regaining some of his original cheerfulness, that quality reminiscent of a well-watered sunflower. He started taking care of himself again, losing weight, rebuilding muscle.

His eyebrows, though—that was the thing. Half of his left eyebrow had turned white despite his youth, and it stayed that color, no matter how he treated his disturbances through better exercise, nicer meals, and romantic relationships. He had to pencil in that area to appear unremarkable in public. A sunflower had spit out its seeds one morning, and someone who had wanted to be its gardener could not recover them.

XI

IT IS FASCINATING to watch someone older and more experienced break down into pained expressions and panting in bed, a
hurting that is a kind of winning. It is the same fascination that
grief-stricken adults exert upon onlooking children at funerals,
except such mourners are now, in a different context with different
people, being pinned down by their younger bedfellows, melting,
sundering into salt, the smell of salt and dung wafting—in one's
hair, tongue, and cavities.

Was Kai still melting like this with others and privately
within? Everything melts around and refracts through Kai, the
perceiver. There are no subplots, only the main arc. It had been a
year and a half since Kai had seen the one whom he had been
wanting to see. Time itself had moved and bent, becoming more
sinuous, stealthy. Its new iterations for Kai did not necessarily
portend an internal change, however. Time was not synonymous
with change. How could Kai have known that years after the day
he had last seen his beloved, years after the year-and-a-half mark
he was presently at, he would still be bothered by his beloved's
memory and by his sense of having been aggrieved by their part-
ing, staring at his own reflection very often as a stranger would?

Kai would often speak to his ex-lover as though that person
were present, even though Kai was alone in a single or partitioned
space. He would entreat that person as he had done back in the day:
Oh, do not do this, severing our thread, oh, oh—and here, Kai would

utter the absentee's name, slightly baffled as he said it because it was becoming more and more curious to remember.

There had been others since who had resembled Kai's ex-lover, but resemblance is not the same as sameness. How could it be? One of them, though, had been a more faithful likeness than the rest. When Kai had looked at his new companion's eyes without peering into them, absorbing that part of his face in isolation, Kai had smiled cryptically at that person, reminded of the one who had left.

What Kai whispered to himself on most nights as he lay in bed was choleric and garbled: *I just want to be normal.* By *normal*, Kai meant his desire not to be abnormal in his unhappiness, in his craving for the brine of that body that had for years now closed itself off to him, having refused him vigorously and with much finality.

How easy it is for a subject to distend into madness, as easy it is to laugh loudly when no one else is even smiling. Someone who is beginning to madden can feel their condition deteriorating, their inner seawall groaning before an incoming masthead that eventually breaks through and lands in coral-colored quicksand at the bottom of a pool, where a long tunnel begins.

An elastic band snaps in the foreground.

Sanity is a rope all too easily dropped.
—Du Fu Soondubu

Be wary of one's mental string breaking, another proverb goes, *for when it does, it cannot be mended back into what it was before the eyes roll back and the whites shine through, altering one's visage.*

Kai felt himself becoming drowsy and enfeebled by his passions again. *I am getting sleepy, Father. Good night.*

The image of his father's face came toward him in return. His father spoke to him in his characteristically gentle way: *You are a naturally happy one, Kai, someone of a cheerful disposition. Where is your fighting spirit? You were never a gloomy one, not really. One must be flexible, emotionally porous, rounded within. No more sighing. It is an unbecoming habit that draws negative attention.*

Kai's father liked circles. His elder son watched fireworks one night through his window after having lain down and gotten back up, while below, others on the sidewalk and in their cars went about the business of living without so much as one look up at the holiday display. The fireworks that ended in circular patterns reminded Kai of an acoustic song regarding someone who draws an oval only to discover that it is their beloved's face: *I drew a circle, and it was thee.*

The oval whom Kai wanted to see the most had once told Kai (after hearing Kai say, *I am someone who has everything*): *But you hate everything you have, and you are a very bitter person.* He had stated this without hiding behind any politic turns of phrase. In this, he was akin to Yoon, who was likewise not shy about speaking of internal matters. While not speaking excessively on principle and by grain, Yoon still had the pleasing habit of never missing a chance to speak when he wanted to. Sudden questions, digressions, and background disturbances would not deter him from his intent if he felt himself committed to it. If the conversation's rhythm was choppy or someone else beat him to the center, this was no missed opportunity for Yoon. He would patiently wait and circle back to finish his point, interrupting the interrupter if need be to say what it was that he most wanted to say with firmness and amiability. Yoon would say whatever it was that he really wanted to say. He would say it. Very little would be kept down and resurface at a later hour.

But why would one not be bitter? Kai thought. *Someone can rarely tell someone else the truth. One cannot call an ugly person ugly, a short person short, a stupid person stupid, ad infinitum.* No one cared to tell Kai that he was pathetic and aging. (Even Jung went silent on this point.) Kai was the only one whose problem it was. For youth was his professional passion. It was youth that Kai wanted: to merge with it, seal it up before a mirror like that stepmother in the fable who lost her mind over poisoned apples. The aging process horrified Kai to the extent that he no longer slept on his side or chest for fear of accruing facial wrinkles.

This is why, Kai grew to realize, whether rightfully or wrongfully, entertainers are tired and drug-addled. The ever-rolling auditioning season, financial instability, and industry-endorsed vanities make an individual abnormal. Such industry parameters incline the spirit to pessimism and an unattractive lugubriousness. Still, Kai would convince himself that his own crusade on behalf of sheer physical charisma was a democratic one. What traverses all walks of life and unites them is the beautiful, the essence of which is discovered in bodies throughout all socioeconomic strata. Kai would insist to himself that beauty was the great leveler, transcending all variables, even as myokymia overtook his left eye for a few days at a time, enhancing his already acute aura of instability.

How could Kai be deemed stable when he was like this? Twisted and sweating in his sheets one night during a month that was not during the peninsula's monsoon season but was still unpleasantly warm, Kai had dreamt that he was facing two windows that were vertically placed centimeters apart in the same wall, with three air-conditioning units mounted on them, and none of these machines were working. In that same dream, the voice of Kai's ex-lover uttered, *I am leaving.*

But you have not been here for years. We are strangers, Kai replied bewilderedly. Voices whooshed in from above and below, culminating in the illusion that Kai's family members were dining together in the living room as he napped in his bedroom, the door of which they had considerately closed. In reality, his bedroom door was wide-open, and no one was there in the house besides him when he awoke to find himself developing a heat rash.

Kai had taken to sleeping with his door open. He had even begun asking his father to keep that door open whenever the latter visited him in his apartment. Alone in his room, whether the door was open or closed, Kai was in the habit of turning his pillow sideways and pushing into its core as he draped one arm around it. He had been accustomed to doing this to his ex-lover's torso.

For the ungenerous, a peninsula is a physical weakling, being a subsidiary landmass that is dependent, by definition, upon a larger landmass for its existence. It is not an island like a continent is but instead a part of an island. It can appear small, like Kai at his smallest when he catches himself reminiscing about bathing with his former lover. That one would complain about wanting to leave the bath as soon as possible. Tutting about how ready he was to leave and not even a little apologetic about this feeling before Kai, who would have been gratified if they could have both shared the bath for a little while longer, he was adamant and so surly about it. *I am done with the bath*, Kai's ex-lover would chirrup. *I am really, truly leaving right now—now, that is right.* Taking the showerhead to rinse off with cooler water, he would wriggle about as Kai sat stiller and let him do as he would before retrieving the showerhead from him to wash his own form in near scalding water, finishing on the coldest setting to emerge alone as a sanded wooden stake.

Time counts for nothing much if one will not allow its tides to do their work. Something within Kai would not let time be time, living in resistance to it. Time became, by Kai's own hand, an insurmountable rampart, and it seemed as though he liked it that way for a little more time. An agitated state of mind would break and set in again every few weeks, at which point Kai would rehearse variations of the same conversation with his ex-lover in his mind.

K: YOU AS A PERSON DO NOT UNDERSTAND THINGS IN THE
RIGHT WAY.

X: IT IS ALL RIGHT TO DISAGREE. NOT EVERYONE HAS TO
AGREE WITH YOU. I AM NOT VIEWING THE SITUATION IN
THE SAME WAY. IT IS NATURAL FOR DIFFERENT
PERSONALITIES TO VIEW MATTERS VERY DIFFERENTLY.
EACH MEASURES OUT THEIR OWN SACRIFICES WITH
PRECISION, EVERYONE ELSE'S WITH INSENSITIVITY. THE
HIGH ROAD ONLY EVER SEEMS TO BE OCCUPIED BY A SINGLE
TRAVELER: ONESELF. EVERYONE TENDS TO THINK OF
THEMSELF AS HAVING BEEN GENEROUS AND HIGH-MINDED,
OTHERS AS HAVING COARSELY PRESSED THEIR ADVANTAGE.

K: I am very lonely.

X: I hope you are doing well.

K: Why do you keep repeating that?

But Kai's former lover was not incorrect. What else is there to say in the aftermath of this kind of an awkward situation?

How could Kai be so distracted by the past when the present was so strange and sudden? Just this week, there had been a mother who had exhorted her son who had just stabbed her in the neck with a pair of scissors after she had berated him for watching television all day: *Flee the scene before the police arrive, my darling.* In another headline, two children, a sister and a brother, had drowned during a thunderstorm when Seoul's waters gurgled up by at least a meter without warning, covering a sewage drain opening that had been left uncovered earlier that day during construction hours. The girl, a decade of age, had fallen through, and her brother, a boy of seven, very bravely and stupidly jumped in after her. She was drowning, and her brother drowned as well while trying to save her, going after her with a great shout. No one in the neighborhood heard any shouting at the time because rain had been falling so aggressively. His rescue mission turned into a little suicide. It was not even a dog's death for them both but an ant's.

An ant stops moving anticlimactically. There is nothing momentous about its death, just as there was no fanfare surrounding a near centennial woman's death recently. She began cursing at her son and her daughter-in-law (who were themselves in their seventies), suspicious that the soup they had presented to her for dinner was not freshly made but culled from leftovers, which could only be the dirtiest of affronts considering how well aware her son was of her poor health. In a cantankerous mood all throughout her meal, she died four hours later in her sleep. Her story is not as sad as another story, in which a father suffocated one of his twin daughters with a towel. The two babes were lying in their crib. Both, the bigger one in particular, would not stop crying. In his fatigue gathered from the office that week, the father came in and dropped a white towel over both of his daughters to mute the noise, returning to his bedroom afterward to nap. His wife had gone out for the day. It was a weekend. Little did he know as he was lying asleep that the towel had clogged the larger twin's airways. She was suffocating. She stopped breathing because the towel was muffling her nostrils and mouth. Her larger body shielded her littler sister from dying, as it created a pocket of air between the sheet and her sister's face. The towel had not been draped over the littler one as tightly, as the larger one had inadvertently created a tent with her body.

That is what life is: life is all this and a father moaning over his child's memory at a funeral that was not his child's but his co-worker's, this co-worker having been someone who had been kind to his child during the child's last months.

For such times as these, Kai turned to proverbs from Buddhist, shamanic, folkloric, scholarly, pop-cultural, and idiomatic sources to tide him over, adapting at will whatever appealed to him at different times of the day. Anything that lifted his spirits and prevented him from remaining a puff pastry of depression for too long was eagerly received and remembered well enough.

Among Kai's favorites were the following:

> The bawling infant gets the nursemaid.
> —Unknown

> If one wants more things to happen,
> they will happen; if one wants less, the
> less there is. Work is one of those things
> that redoubles and shrinks at will. One
> keeps oneself as busy or not as one is
> inclined to be.
> —The *Myeongsim Bogam*

> Just because one is hungry does not
> mean that one need stoop to eating
> animal droppings. There are limits.
> —Unknown

> They are overwintered.
> —A cluster fly specialist

> The happy are healthy, the sad sickly.
> What does that make mental yo-yoers?
> —Lisa Lee

> The pebble that was taken to be a pearl
> was a pebble.
> —Min

A precious stone, even if muddied and
worn, will shine out from a sea of rubble.
—MIN

Depending on the day, the same
igneous formation can be labeled a pebble,
a pearl, a diamond, or whatnot. People are
moody and fickle.
—MIN

Change is immune to change.
—A YOKO ONO IMPERSONATOR

The loaf has yet again collapsed in
the oven.
—HUR YOUNG-IN

Sometimes the grass is greener. If it
is more fun over there, go over there. It
was more fun over there than over here, so
a certain sage moved locations—verdant,
verdant change!
—HWANG JINI

No one watches the other nor cares.
The fear of public humiliation remains
an egoist's fantasy. One should be so
lucky that the public would look up

and pay enough attention to point
and smile unkindly.
—SEO TAIJI

Remember where you buried your infant
and where you are: this is a gas station.
—A YONSEI UNIVERSITY NURSE

Two friends had gone carousing by the
Han. One returned, the other did not. Is
this friendship?
—A KBS NEWSCASTER

Do not block the bus that is arriving or the
one that is departing from the station. Or
was it a train? Do not hinder the straying
or stand in the way of new arrivals.
—YOSUKE KUBOZUKA

Do not turn into a mild public nuisance.
—KANG HO-DONG

A monarch butterfly was brushed off
someone's knee without proper deference
(and probably fatally crippled in the
process) because it was mistaken for a
mosquito. It was not like its spiritual
cousin, a quality knife, that cut through

the pouch that encircled it. So keen was its
blade that it was never at risk of being
unrecognized or handled incorrectly.
—KIM DU-HAN

*Dawn will arrive even though we twist
the crowing rooster's neck. Even if we
crack that fowl dead, gripping its head
round and round, the sun will rise.* Former
president Kim Young-Sam uttered these
crudely literal words for a cheerful effect.
Both that cock and the day have broken.
—A YTN JOURNALIST

XII

UNLIKE FOR HUMANS, crawling out of one's shell is not a good thing for hermit crabs. The act promises death. A prince among hermit crabs that one of Kai's friends owned grew depressed over the course of a few weeks after it was gifted to that friend by another friend. The prince's accompanying companion had perished in their shared tank. His new owner tried somewhat halfheartedly to revive the prince's spirits by performing a few prescribed correctives: cleaning the plastic tank and placing enough water in it (although it never lacked water to begin with, so Kai's friend replaced what water there was with bottled water). Kai's friend did not, however, purchase a replacement companion for the prince to consort with. There were no fresh princesses, fellow noblemen, or commoners for the prince to pincer with. Nor did the owner enlarge the prince's living quarters, adjust the tank's humidity levels, or pour more sand into the prince's kingdom. The crab aquarium was not relocated to the base of a yellow mountain where the prince could burrow into many sands and molt with leisure. Growing more pensive each day despite his owner's redoubled efforts, the prince strayed outside of his shell—first a pincer tip, then antennae, eyes, a few legs, abdomen, and remaining legs, until it was sitting a few centimeters away from its shell entirely, staring expressionlessly upward into the cage's artificial light. What a despondent prince this was. Kai's friend experienced not a little guilt when it became clear that the prince had keeled over, having shriveled into a cross between a dried prune and a worm used for fish bait. Let this be a parable about the dangers of allowing crustaceans to experience unease. The aristocratic ones are a crusty bunch. Beware when buying them as domestic treats. Crawling out of one's shell is not always a good thing.

So why did Kai do it? Breaking character does not bode well for his type. It was not that he could never alter his patterns, only that certain situations were to be avoided when there was an intuition that some deed would be perilously unrewarded. That is the tricky part: knowing what to do when and where to whom. Lives are lived in aircraft that do not always orbit on cue. Min was well and fine. Why had Kai felt compelled to invite him over that day?

You changed your face. It must have been expensive, Kai said wryly. They were in Kai's apartment. Min's home was squalid enough that it would have been an embarrassment for both host and guest to have met there. Kai was laughing at Min. They were meeting for the first time in over a year, and Min had somehow managed to smuggle in some plastic surgery in this interval. He had had his eyelids cut in the Western fashion. When his eyes were open, he resembled a double-lidded amphibian. The bridge of his nose had been heightened and his jaw shaved to give his face a more feline look. His hair was newly layered, straightened, dyed. Where had he found the money to do all this? Why, where he always had: through sheer cunning, gambling, thrift, and borrowing from gullible friends and pitying relatives. He looked like himself, just better. Not good enough for strangers to buy off his nights but enough for them to tell him that the expense was worth it. Min was not a diamond but a pebble.

This pebble was a strange one. It liked to be swallowed, not sucked. It had had more than the usual number of near-death experiences. As a third grader, Min had gone up to his apartment villa's roof with some of his neighborhood friends, hopping onto its cement ledge. It was about thirty centimeters wide. The group watched him hoist himself onto it. They looked on as he started walking on the roof's balustrade, dangling one foot over the other, miming tightrope-walking. A couple minutes in, a faint shout could be discerned. A woman from the opposite apartment block had spotted the children as she was hanging laundry on her balcony. She began pointing and cursing, scurrying over to haul them off the roof, prevent them from playing such reckless games. The whole time, she did not cease yelling about their lunacy. *What are you thinking? Is no one afraid in your generation? Your parents will be furious.* She yanked ears and herded everyone off the roof, which was permanently locked thereafter. *She has ruined everything*, Min sadly thought at the time and promptly forgot about it afterward.

Roofs are roofs, and they are not the only things that can end a person. Cars can as well. Around a decade ago, Min had almost tasted death when he crossed a street without waiting for the proper light. He could have sworn that there were no cars coming. He was only trying to bypass a clogged lane that was slow-moving. But as soon as he crossed the first lane and was about to enter the second, a silver bullet came out of nowhere, speeding a centimeter before Min's nose. So close was it that the draft around it had touched Min's face. The jaywalker had felt that gust moving inside him. Min trembled whenever this memory overtook him— whether from fear or anticipation, it was uncertain.

More than anyone, Min felt that he knew Kai best. Did anyone know Min? Did anyone want to? Min often thought to himself: *Jung trivializes whatever Kai feels. Only I have the right to do that.* Sitting in Kai's living room with him, Min could feel it: that Kai believed he was beyond the point where other people's hardships could grant perspective to his own. *Min tells me I am fine*—Min could see Kai thinking as they were sitting. *I am fine, you are fine, we are fine, the world is altogether fine*—Min could see Kai mentally repeating.

(Why do you grind your teeth almost every night, dearest Kai?)

Why did Kai care about being looked at through Min's eyes— Min the Malingerer who spent all his beer money on card games, arcades, computer tournaments, and touching up his face? Well, Min had always watched Kai, and Kai performed well under his gaze. Min thought as he watched Kai rearranging certain trifles on his coffee table, pausing every so often before going to look for beer glasses, that Kai took pleasure in being watched, and that that was why he kept moving. *Kai thinks*, Min thought like Jung thought, *that he is such a catch—attractive, lecherous, guarded, immodestly embittered—but is he in actuality? Just look at him, still ridiculously waiting for his old self to come back as though life had lingered in wait. How pathetic that Kai still dreams about his greatest darling, about how he lost his temper at him for arriving late for supper, chastising that person without pausing for breath as he shut all the doors around them. Meanwhile, the latecomer tried to explain that he had been running late due to some training workshop. The more he tried to explain himself, the more doors kept appearing that Kai had to shut, the last one opening into a room where Han was listening. How pathetic. All that waiting for that particular lover to come to him made Kai funny in the head. He still cannot stop* tee-hee-hee*ing about his master classes in conversation. How stupid to utter such things with one's own mouth. That is probably why Kai's favorite left him: he was tired of this, of Kai as a person and sex partner.*

In Kai's head, Kai could hear Min calling out to him, *Come meet me by the fig tree past the azaleas. Wait for me there. But what are you waiting for, Kai, my friend? I wonder what kind of a second coming is in the works for you, you who say with your hands covering your face:*

> Coming
>
> not coming
>
> coming
>
> coming
>
> not coming
>
> I lost it
>
> coming
>
> come
>
> come here
>
> come by
>
> come forever
>
> get covered in it
>
> now
>
> not now
>
> coming
>
> come now
>
> come to me

keep going

keep going

keep going

keep going

keep going.

Could Kai take it? Min wanted to ask (in his own head now, not anymore in Kai's). It was best not to think too deeply about such things, to just keep moving until one could not do so anymore. *Go kill yourself,* Kai had merrily instructed Min once. Min had shot back, *You would feel sorry if I really did it.*

Was Kai truly lost or milking the bottle to milk Min?

What did Kai's apartment look like? It looked like Kai. And Kai kept insisting that he was tired of living these days, so Min, Min himself reflected, should oblige Kai, reduce the terrain of Kai's body to burnt grass, a landscape where people share the ontological status of plants. To Min's chagrin, Kai never looked at him seriously, even though Min was striking in his own way. Kai dismissed Min, as Min never seemed to say anything very, very interesting. Plus, Min was dropping out of Kai's life the more he surrounded himself with seedier underworld types. Min was not simply having intercourse with the lower classes but falling into them himself in Kai's opinion.

How did it happen? Min shoved Kai at a certain point after following him into the bathroom when Kai needed to empty his bladder after having drunk multiple glasses of a liquid that ran clear without being water. Kai hit his forehead on the tub. *Kai, are you awake? Are you there? Can you wake up for me?* Min pleaded beside the still bough. As Min wrung his hands, he unbuttoned his pants and entered an unconscious Kai. Was Kai only pretending to be asleep? After Min brought himself to a finish while kneading Kai's neck, entreating Kai to show him something, he backed away on his knees and burst out sobbing. Whatever did Min do with Kai's body?

And then, and then—Kai's body was never found. Whatever happened to him remained unknown, an ellipsis that destroyed his parents. Or was Kai fine, merely living in seclusion with his family's blessings? Was Kai's fall in the bathroom a ploy to capture more of his brother's affections? Was Min the epilogue that tied all these different spools together before the commencement of another great war? Kai was not unhappy anymore. Min giggled.

Whose story was this—had it always been Han's? One of Han's last outlines had been for a novella about the collapse of the North. *A new generation of men and women unsuccessfully fight for peace, leaving the peninsula a watery crater as the price of their collective failure. The population in that area of the world sinks to a quarter of its original size. Yet another orphaned generation waits for the seasons to change.* Min chattered on and on, both seriously and glibly as he sat before his mirror at home, stroking his facial alterations.

In Min's memory, that night had decomposed into a series of polite evasions, with both parties glossing over his sameness over the decades because Min himself was disappointed by it rather than proud.

Min was not considered normal given his morbid imaginative life. But neither was he considered indecently strange. He was considered somewhere in between. He kept himself unoccupied, and this excess of leisure time exacerbated his natural vindictive streak. No one knew anything about his parents. His extended relatives were not well-off, but they had enough to placate Min when he snorted and bucked for money during the holidays. Han, when he was tired and bored, would every so often send Min a little something out of his pocket. (At this time, Han was still alive. When he left, Min forgot about him.) Min did not think about Kai that much despite their recent meeting. Thoughts may drift around, but they eventually return to their owner. The universe is claimed by mirrors ever straining to reflect themselves, chains of narcissus flowers, and petals praying to fall back toward the stem in perpetuity.

Min leaned over the sink. He leaned in so closely that his pupils almost touched the mirror's glass. The magnified perspective was making him slightly nauseous. Brown patches, ovals that elongated, coils, and dust flecks moved across his corneas. *I am a fancy car, the fanciest of cars—and the one who torches them. Forget the televised eaters who name themselves after car brands. I defy them all, am the eagle at the summit.*

Most of the surgically altered dislike not being looked at. The same applied to Min. He was strange but not an alien being. He had once overheard Kai snickering about his mediocre body and face, and that was that, part of the end for Min. Min saw and emulated things, and emulators are the most dangerous kind of characters. They have no limits. Nothing is sacred. When the envious envy, everyone around them should tremble. For envy and resentment are the primary causes behind grand thefts and slaughters. Min had a habit of tracing his scalpel marks with his thumbs. This motion, along with the way he would run his knuckles across his upper lip, made people uncomfortable.

Cows wander from their steep grazing pastures to sit by the sea, chewing their cud away from their ranchers. Theirs is the peaceful, vacant feeling that Kai must be experiencing now, asleep and unaware of what is happening. Jung had a better grasp of what was happening. Jung had a better grasp than Kai did of what had happened between him and Min the night the latter had visited Kai's apartment. She was not a cow taking a walk by a seaside cliff but a proactive being who was not opposed to treading water. Water can taste sweet, and so can gusts of cold air encountered while walking up a snowy mountain.

Jung had had a baby, not fathered by her ex-fiancé but another man who was now her husband. They had met and finalized their marriage in half a year. Compatibility is an elusive thing. Usually, one of the two is a bit rounder in energy, a bit softer, more pleasant, forgiving in demeanor, somewhat patient, and not prodding. Jung and her husband had met and understood each other, forging a rapport that was appropriate for people of their age, experience, and socio-economic background. Neither was in it simply to be married, as if marriage were a national sport that individuals mastered according to the number and quality of their offspring and the wealth they accumulated together.

Jung and her husband did not agree with this attitude toward marriage. They had both endured significant personal and professional hardships and wanted someone to create a life with—a work of art that would endure while they were alive and fade away with grace when they did. They wanted a peaceful yet exciting thing in itself. They found it together and acted swiftly. Their only child was conceived without much preparation. His birth had been difficult: Jung was one of the few who had sobbed on all fours from the sensations effected by her induction medicine. It was what it was. Things are what they are. They remain as is, which is to say that no one knows how a marriage will change from one moment to the next.

Jung had a better sense of what happened because she shared words with Kai a few days after Min had visited him. Kai was not limping or acting funny. It did not appear as though he had endured a major concussion or minor brain damage. There were no stitches. She had come over to Kai's apartment that evening to eat and drink nice things. The apartment looked the same, neither neater nor more disorganized than it had ever been. It looked like Kai. What was natural stayed natural. He was not stretching or staring about desolately. He was slicing what Jung had requested by the counter. He was not looking at Jung strangely nor was she looking at him that way. Min might as well have no longer existed for Kai. That was how infrequently Kai's thoughts turned to Min and their night together. For Min had not touched Kai. Min had wanted to, Kai surmised, but he had only made eyes at Kai, growing pensive and slightly distracted as their conversation ripened. It is difficult to request things in person when one is unsure of the answer. Min had been wise in not asking Kai for anything since Kai would not have given it. Min just kept looking at Kai in the same way that Kai sometimes looked at Jung when thinking about their younger days. *Oh, Kai*, she would sigh whenever she caught him looking at her like this, a little strangely, sadly. *Oh, Kai!*

Go away, Jung—suddenly, even her friendly presence irritated Kai. He sent her off emphatically. She felt the atmosphere dip and excused herself. Who cares whether the two had a scuffle in Kai's apartment? Min had written to her that he felt guilty about it, but only Kai's parents and perhaps his brother on a good day would care to draw out the details from Kai in this state.

Kai had the urge to cook an elaborate meal as soon as she left. What would he make? Something for his brother, yes, and Jung's husband. Kai was not psychologically stable then, with his moods rising and falling several times in a single day. He tried to focus on cooking a stew for at least twenty minutes until he gave up and began wondering what else he could do on such a weeknight. He could force himself to go back to cooking, but whoever popularized the notion that cooking is a soothing activity was backward in his estimate. Cooking was not soothing him at that moment, becoming yet another aggravating stimulant.

What can one do when one feels querulous in the early evening, when the night still holds possibilities, but the prospect of leaving one's house feels burdensome? Humans are funny. When they are indoors, they want to be let out; when they go outside, they whine about wanting to be let back in. Kai was bored and annoyed with his acquaintances, yet he did not want to rest at home. *Let me pretend to be Min; that should do the trick. His fantasies and actions are one, so intertwined are they. That is why he is dangerous, is to be held at bay: he acts out his dreams in the act of dreaming. A blade of grass is straightened and shorn in one stroke. His body leaps before his mind has determined in which direction. This quality was exciting when we were younger. Is that the case now?* Kai contemplated.

Min was already outside beneath the moonlight that night. He was walking away from a house that was similar to the hairdresser's, a house that he shared with his landlady's family, a male university student, and a female nurse. When he entered a PC room, Min failed to draw attention to himself despite paying handsomely for it. Inside the computer arcade, he picked up a cup of instant noodles and walked over to an unoccupied station. He played a role-playing game for eight hours straight. Although he had never trained with small sandbags slung over the backs of his hands to steady them, he could click rapidly without his fingers cramping. One index finger would keep clicking while the other hand funneled noodles into his mouth, which slurped and hurled profanities through the microphone at precocious elementary schoolers who were bungling his virtual quests. Min had more kills than defeats. He felt nicely emptied of depths—a shiny surface.

With increasing frequency these days, Kai wanted to live as Min did. Kai had been wanting that for a while now. To live for nothing—what a sentiment. To be a cow staring out into the gray ocean. Kai could be envious of another's lackadaisical attitude, where beer money and gaming time were all that mattered. Whatever about Min bothered Kai, Kai left alone between them. And Kai resolved not to see Min anymore. What had happened happened. The air between them had grown unpleasant.

It is time to go hermit crab hunting with Yoon, Kai silently declared. Yoon had just returned from another trip to Okinawa, and now there he was, sitting on a bench by the sea in Busan, looking out at the horizon. A few hours later, he repeated this activity indoors, looking out at the waters from a coveted table in a hotel restaurant. A few hours after this meal, he was back at the shore, chatting with Kai about all the subjects that started with a certain letter as part of a game that he and Kai had begun playing decades ago, giggling together like lovably pudgy children. Those from Yoon's and Kai's pasts went unmentioned. Both friends were elated to spend time together again. Yoon picked up the pins of their long-running conversations with confidence. Everything in his hands became a treat. Kai reported his little deaths with various figures while smirking. Yoon nodded along without being disingenuous. When Kai confided that he had met someone special, Yoon listened without looking at Kai's face, turning toward the sea again, chewing on his inner cheeks. Both figures watched an elderly woman push a cart filled with cardboard boxes up a hill and disappear from sight.

Shall we walk?

Yes, let us walk; by all means, let us.

You know there are no hermit crabs out here in the winter, Kai. Even if it was the summer season, this is the busiest beach in Busan. Those poor little things would not stand a chance, could never play tag out here with their pincers.

Oh, is that so? I did not look into it. They just sounded like a nice excuse to see you, Yoon-shi, Yoo-oon, Yoon-Yoon. I wanted to scuttle around this wintry beach, be hermit crabs together.

You are being quite cute tonight. Did you work at it? Why, you are glowing, very much so.

They frolicked on the beach, exclaiming over how the season was not as frigid as it had been in years past. They jostled each other after buying separate bags of steaming walnut pockets. Most would have been inclined to share a bag to avoid overeating and to stoke a feeling of camaraderie, but Yoon and Kai's friendship was bolstered by jabs about how everyone should have their own bag—none of that garbage about sharing bags, whittling down portions. It was the highest achievement to feel full instead of filling out empty courtesies.

But the rumors, Yoon murmured as they walked along the boardwalk that was bustling with performers despite the rising wind. Music trickled everywhere as college students, a few high schoolers, and full-time street performers invited donations without outright panhandling.

But the rumors—*what rumors? Ah, yes.* Kai cracked his neck. *Yoon, they are like all rumors, half-true, half-not.*

Yoon said nothing, only giving Kai a strange look, one that seemed to lengthen by the minute as they continued walking. This look did not make Kai feel defensive, although he had already recognized that no matter what he said, Yoon would not take his words at face value. Yoon shifted his gaze as he bit into another walnut ball filled with red bean jam. They kept walking, not as briskly but still brisk enough. Yoon was not looking anywhere specifically, just not at Kai, while Kai's gaze remained on Yoon all throughout, with brief flits to the side whenever a nearby musician began singing in the bittersweet French chanson style. The wooden boardwalk did not seem to have an end that night. It had changed somehow. It kept going.

What are you thinking, Kai? Yoon asked without rushing.

I was thinking of my brother.

No.

What do you mean by no, Yoon?

That is not what the rumors suggested. Stop that. What are you talking about? Yoon walked out onto one of the piers built in an area well before where the boardwalk ended. Yoon could hear Kai scurrying after him, with the paper bag in Kai's hand crinkling loudly as he crushed its opening to prevent its contents from falling out. The pastries had gone cold, and so had Yoon. He really could not understand Kai sometimes—was having trouble stomaching the sight of Kai just then. There were no musicians, food vendors, or pedestrians around them anymore to shield Kai from Yoon's bewilderment. What was Kai babbling about? He was assuming such ridiculous poses when Han was whispering that Kai had disgraced Min in a very particular way that day they had met in Kai's apartment, and Min had let Kai because Min was strange and a stranger to everyone.

On the pier, Yoon felt its wooden boards creaking under his feet as the world fell away from him. He experienced himself billowing out to engulf the sky and sea, subsuming these elements under his system of anthropomorphic relations as an unfeeling god would even as he underwent an implosion, collapsing into a beam at the same time. He was unfurling like an obsidian sail even as he was shrinking into a legless starfish, a thimble struggling to avoid becoming crushed by the waves that would pound it into gravel under the pier.

What was wrong with his friend Kai? Why was he even friends with Kai to begin with? Had Kai always been such a crooked branch, or had he deteriorated after some self-aggrandized disappointment? When Kai opened his mouth to say something else, Yoon's impatience spilled out onto the night like hot oil, and he hit Kai across the mouth, not very hard but not softly either. Kai did not venture another word. The two stood on the pier and looked out at the blackness that was not as black as it could have been because of the lights emitted from the shore, which were nonetheless preferable to the image of deserted cliffs for both onlookers—sheer stone slabs rising one after another that would repel even lichen. They looked out into the well-illuminated darkness in silence, then returned to the boardwalk without speaking. They did not meet again for a while until they did.

XIII

[Excerpts from Yoon's correspondence with his foreign high school friends over the years]

I'M IN THE train station and I just saw a KP girl walk by who would have made you cry. diamond earring, tiny fauxhawk, black leather jacket, and a face that looked like she could watch a puppy shoot a kitten and her only response would be to take another ciggy puff

*

bro, i need to get my dick outta the sandbox and into a cactus.

*

dude, i need the omelet.
i need some pretzels and the body pillow.

*

WHAT IS WRONG WITH A FIRECROTCH? Nothing, let me tell you. as a people, we are FIRE.

*

i like writing emails/letters cuz i can gather all my thoughts &
take my time to say em exactly teh way i want
without leaving stuff out or going overboard/underboard

*

Rabid dogs punch themselves out in the long run

*

Hug?

*

1) ur a dog
2) ur an asshole
3) u got asshole problems
4) so i love u!!!!!

love
the token nice friend

*

저는 수업 시간에 난 . . . 나는;)하지만 당신이 그리워요
잠 좀 자자! 놈 후반 !!
키스!
당신의 동성애 연인

*

Medusa!!!
Nice!!!
Next yr I wanna be either a flamenco dancer or a flamingo

*

Much love,
canadian fruitball

*

Korean vs octopus

*

She wants to feed you asado again.

*

If you are feeling shrivelled my loving and precious squid, then
stay hydrated and stay positive ... You know better than to not
moisturize!! ...

*

How goes it?
Baby bite

*

lifelustfreedom

*

Dont give up our fight on the squid - just dont break my heart like that
Baby bite

*

good pep talk my child
good pep talk

penis,
bush

*

America, Friends, Countrymen
I did not have sexual relations with that Korean (in the house
of lords).

Love,
Slick Willy

*

you both signed on and chatted me at the same time. let me show
you what you wrote.

Kai: zup boo

Yoon: sup foo
please stop having sex with each other.
thank you

*

you are such a stank one you . . .

*

Got a new celly #?
Gimme your address?
I saw the new movie we talked bout yesterday. It was a fecal movie.
But you're a fecal, fecal man!

*

balls
i feel like i fucked this one up/// . . . i didnt know how to juggle
two bitches at once and pissed off both wifey and mistress . . .

clinton fucked it up too . . .

*

ROAR

*

hugs =) and much forbidden love

*

Yoon, me misses you . . .
its dark and cold and lonely in shinchon w.o tender bulglgi and
kimchizzle . . .
there you are
i knew you would come

*

Dearest nasty nast

beeeep.. me misses u

Warmest regards,
mr Sheep

*

Listen Yoon!!
I love you sooooo much:) Of cause as a fiend.
Hehehe~
Then you comming class,I can enjoooooy~!!!!

*

Hi Yoon!! I'm still working now, but I want to ask you How do you think and which one better??

And thank you for message:D I have a dark past, so I don't have much to say about myself.

It makes everyones feel down, Ahahaha!!

But I want to talk with you more,I continue study & practice English!!

*

Yoon thank you sooooo much..

I always encouraging by your words. Your words are knocks me out than any words.

I love you so much.

Hmm..Iike you wouldn't believe I wonder why you cant find good fulltime job yet, I only know your good points . . . to be honest, your bad point is sometime you tease me and drink beer a lot . . . ? lol

Rejection letters from companies?

I dont like use Email like this situation. Sometime exchange emails, likely to cause misunderstanding. Face to face is the best . . . Many asian pepole try to do things in an insidious way. I hate that kind of person.

I feel you are tird . . . I never see unnerve your confidence:'(

You can lose confidence in a while, but its not your life. You are so smart, kind and strong. The best man . . . I'd rather not say . . . lol

You will be alright:) I know. Im so sorry for cant say well. I wish I
could speak English more better..
Yes Yoon! Do your best!!

.......You havent changed a bit, still handsome Im jealous!
Mabe kimch power?
I eat kimuch everyday now, because I found good tast one but I
got more gray hairs . . . too late? Haaaa:0
Almost 8years since we met? No wonder I've become old:)

I accept some incidents and feel clam these days, feel any emothion
akin to resign for my life. Mabe little bet tird but its ok, rainy days
never stay.

Noooo Yoon san! I love bicycle x)
I will buy new one yeah:D
Early morning, I feel wendy so comfortable!! Ahahahaha~!!!!

And . . . yeah I cant understand about Ai.
She still want to kiss me. I still love her but I dont care anymore
about love. It makes me tird.
You know Im happy whatever she dont love me lol

I changed hospital, new hospital is little bet far for me right now.
But good hospital:) Old doctor said me you should stay in bed.
Muscle training? Nonono.
And new doctor said what are you doing, you should move your neck!
They told me about neck already stiff and misaligned!
He got mad at me, I feel O~M~G~ . . . lol

They made me schedule for rehabilitation:)
Hard rehabilitation will be start end of Jun, aiyaia~:(
And will use TCI for my ear. Finaly, take a stap foward . . .

Yoon? Take your time, take it easy.

*

Hi Yoon san:)
How are you? Im so sorry for late:(
You quit job . . . OMG I respect the way you act very fast!

My heart always say thank you to you.
You give me much strength everytime whatever you are . . .
you always care of me that feeling is enough for me, your words is
always uplifting:)
I wanna be like you for all . . .

OMG you still play at night? lol
Ahaha I cant do that anymore lol Its not joking right?!

Did you get good Kimchi at Korean town?
Korean Kimch and Chainese Kimch is diffrent? When I worked
with Chainese, thay made Kimch by there self. Can you make it??
American pepole asked me can you make Sushi? before.
Mabe my question is similar to that lol
Hmm . . . sometime sex is very important for us, we have the four
primitive fountains . . . me too, no sex but you have wife, there is
nothing I haveeee!!

Just jelly ... ('Д') lo
And ... Congratulations*\(^^)/* You are my white hair mate from now!

I have some news.

My family came to my house on that day, they cook and clean the house for me and I went to ENT. Doctor just gave me 88medicines and said me you should come again 1month later. I thought take medicines and get better? No, there is no point doing that.

And then I threw my all medicine away and had a row with my family.

And then my family worrie about me, so me and my family talked with doctor again.

She looks like bother and she said medicines does not work for you anymore, you cant fix your ear, cant do anything. But if you wanna try something you can go hearing aid store at Shinjyuku. But I dont know it will work for you.

You know, I feel much down and I ask her so why you gave me the medicines, why should I keep comming here. For what?

Also my family up set, I should find another ENT. Should change again.

Now I wear hearing aid ...

And about orthopedic surgery, the program was warms the neck then get massages, muscle training. Yes, stretch and lift things(1kg ... lol).

But I fall and scrape my face about 3week ago ... ofcourse I was land on my hands but my muscle weakness so I couldnt carry the weight of my body. For this reason that started weight training for my arm too.I fell for the first time in years . . .

Last week, I finaly could open the bottle caaaaps:'(

I took about 15min for open the cap before the rehabilitation but I never thought itd be this happy to open the cap.

I hope you never know that the moment bottle makes a sounds, I feel like hit the jack pot with slot machines at casino.

I was realy happy, and I was try 4times more after I got home . . . lol

A right handed squeeze of 13.6kg, left hand is 0kg. Isnt it funny? lol Im such a dork but what I am now. But my body got much better than before with even this:)

One step then one more step. Thats good enough for now . . . mabe:)

And last Saturday I went to my workplace for talk with head nurse about hows my body going and what should I do later etc . . .

I went to there for the first time in a very long while, so I was a little nervous, but they were very warmly welcome me. They gave me a big hug(Here is not US, nobody do hug but) and then encourages me or amuses me . . . each of them has big love and compassion, its a very wonderful work site thats why I love my workplace and workmates.

And my dear nurse gave me a charm against evil lol

Head nurse said me, you cant work at July, I know you always do your best. If you start work now, your body will cry huh? We are waiting for you, no problem. Break your leg for rehabilitation.

Some Japanese co cut pepole whatever got accident. I know I cant work now but I was so scary about it.

I was happy and almost cry. Im easily moved to tears no matter how much time passes.
Sad and cry, frustrate and cry, happy then cry . . . ahaha(^^)

Oh! Did you meet with Kai!?
Im thinking about Im gonna quite delivery job. They waiting me too but cant do anymore . . . If I will do by my self, my hearing aid will get problem.

I will sent you pictures later too!! We still young:)
Awaaa . . . I think I made spelling mistake lol My Japanese is no good, English too, where am I from??
And you tell me about you more, you dont have to so worrie about me:)

*

Yoon san! So sorry for late (><;)
How are you doing?Are you ok now?
Please give me your adress. I'v got something for you.
And I wrote to you . . . long love letter lol
I wanna sent you when I have a time:)

[Translated from the original Korean, a letter by Yoon sent to his ex-wife during their courtship period]

I did not know that writing a letter was such a difficult thing. Yesterday, today, I called you, but your roommate answered.

That I suddenly gave you a call is not necessarily a good thing, I agree. However, have you given thought to why I would do such a thing? Judging from your tone over the phone, it seemed that you were disappointed in me, but where have these feelings come from? I did something wrong, but was it so wrong? Were my actions that irresponsible? In brief, what did I do to make you question even my character? (Am I misreading you here?)

In your mind, after reading these words, you may still think me arrogant, but if that were true, why would I write a letter like this?

Of course, there were many problems with my actions. But let me give a short explanation. At the time, my circumstances were such that I had to. I hope you can understand that right now.

Understanding or whatever else aside, if you ask me why you are obligated to receive these kinds of letters from me, I do not have anything to say. But at the very least, I thought this far, felt this much, so when I found out your phone number, I called you and then wrote you this letter.

Already, in the middle of not having met each other in a year and a half, you must have changed—even if not a lot, at least a little.

When I think about such things, I really wonder whether I am doing the right thing. If this is all a mistake, if you feel I am someone who is unrelated to you at all, I apologize for these actions of mine.

But regardless of how you see things, I do not feel I am someone who cannot tell you these things.

In truth, in our past phone conversations, I feel that I showed you my intent. I say this because (regardless of whether you accept my meaning or not) I do not feel that this is excessive. (You would say that I am being willful.) You may have stated your position and meaning over the phone, but it was difficult to say for me.

It feels like my words are going in aimless circles. In any case, the you I think of is someone who can tell the other your feelings, and the me you know is someone who can listen to your meaning without anxiety.

We have been apart for too long for me to expect something drastically immediate, and both of us are not in any position to do so. But if you are unwilling to think about the future together—in other words, if you are uncomfortable about having a connection with me in the present with the future in mind—at the very least deliver that purpose to me. I said it before, but I trust I am someone who can ask that much. Besides, I have not done anything good here. How could I pester you any further?

And this is probably a simple misunderstanding, but I get the feeling that you are avoiding me, and there is no need for you to do so. I wish you would take into consideration my own self-esteem as a person. (Maybe this is the thing that impelled me to write this letter.) To sum everything up, I would like for you to give us the chance to have a serious conversation. If that is not possible, if I have too many problems for that, you can at least send me word of that, right?

I would be thankful if you could give me a call as soon as you receive this letter.

PS: This is my phone number. (If I am not there, if you leave a message, I will call you even if it is late.)

(You may feel taken aback by this question:) is marrying me really an impossibility? Me? Am I really a forgotten person? Please marry me.

PPS: After I wrote that letter, something felt insipid, so I am taking up my pen again. Even now it appears as though you trust your instinct that I was not clear about our relationship before I left Seoul because I took you lightly. But at the time, was it normal to drag you into everything when I myself was unsure of myself in a strange place?

Of course, one could say that relationships are about enduring hardships together, that that is what is most important. This could be a counter-argument, but even now I do not regret not committing what was between us then in stone. In a situation where I had no confidence in providing for you, well, what must I have done?

(Were you really sure about me then?) If there is a better route than myself, a path that I could see you taking for your own good, do you think it would be fair of me to take you down a worse road?

If you ask me whether I think my circumstances have improved from a year and a half ago, I cannot give you a decisive answer. Yet have not things changed from before? Anyway, it was from such thoughts that I asked to stay in touch before. Of course, that proposal was dashed at your hand; you had your reasons from your position.

This attitude that I had toward you is something you must not have liked, but I am that kind of person. Love is something to be realized, and as one lives, one keeps living. But must we get married in that way—live like that?

If there is someone who can give you happiness from a better position (and no doubt there is), I will withdraw without saying two words. Of course, I felt at the time you had no conviction about me.

Please do not see me as being too practical-minded. Please do not see me as incompetent.

Events have drifted in a strange way, but that was because my condition was unstable back then. Now the question seems to lie in your decision.

Do not take my words to mean that I am forcing a decision from you.

Let us not contact each other at a stage when there is no surety. If there is something a little lukewarm for you as you are trying to judge how you feel about me, even if I stand sure about you, I will sense this myself and withdraw.

After writing for a while, things seem, even in my eyes, to be spinning around here in a rambling way without any clearness. Just one thing: let us not forget that we are in a strange phase of our lives, trying to study. Let us stay true to our aims. And be truthful toward each other.

Yoon

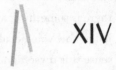

XIV

NEAR THAT SAME beach where Kai and Yoon had walked and fought, around a decade and a half later, Nari was employed in the market district as a pedicurist and occasional manicurist. Clipping and polishing fingers and toes, massaging palms and feet, and applying lotion where needed, the only child of the hairdresser who had toiled for Kai's pleasure was now responsible for the more modest pleasures of her customers in a lower-middling nail salon located where certain stalls never closed. Nari had turned out decently overall, respectful, doe-like, and only a little emotionally crinkled from her childhood.

One of her mother's friends, Kai, had disappeared one day. Kai had come around on a couple of other occasions after that time Nari had made the mistake of running to him for help. She had never known his name. The past came up in clumps for her that were hazy. She could not remember what little there was to remember. It was uncertain whether Kai had sent her family money in the years after he ceased frequenting their house. Such an arrangement did not seem likely considering how her mother had changed. Even the coarsest nighttime positions were no longer available to her mother due to her age and self-inflicted slump.

In high school, Nari had not been the sort to get beaten up. There were no Herculean confrontations between her and her classmates that involved cigarette burns or inventive and vehement cursing. Neither was she unlovingly passed around like a milk bottle for wearing her uniform in provocative ways. Such happenings did not inform her emotional constitution. Finding someone like Kai to support her was not a passion of hers. Unlike her mother, Nari had little interest in becoming the star of her own television channel devoted to the opposite of fasting. She possessed no aspirations to watch others eat or render herself into a sweetmeat. Whatever eating could be done would be done in private and freely. Any money at stake would be present in an abstract sense, as tomorrow's consideration regarding who could be a suitable marriage partner, be able to provide for her and their children, ease the burden of making a living, and save her from developing calluses like her grandmother's.

Her grandmother had continued selling side dishes at one of Seoul's largest night markets. The mother of Nari's mother had not matured into one of those grandmothers on television who collect recyclable cardboard from the street for money all while enduring slights from strangers for undertaking these duties deemed demeaning in popular culture. Her grandmother had not evolved into one of those grandmothers who collect unusable paper materials out of superstition. Her grandmother had not fallen prey to hoarding, arthritis, paranoia, or celibacy. Such ailments were avoided as her grandmother was now only in her fifties and tidy-looking. This grandmother, who had been Nari's knight when she was growing up, had wounded her granddaughter's sensibilities by refusing to visit bathhouses together anymore on the grounds that Nari had flouted her orders not to get tattooed. The younger one now brandished a goldfish tattoo across her entire back and buttocks in the style belonging to the peninsula's underworld groups with which she had no association. This was one of the reasons why Nari had left Seoul for Busan.

Nari was a sweet and proficient worker. She was deferential. Her soft-spoken demeanor pleased and pained a salary-woman who entered the shop one day. This professional arrived for her appointment in an unassuming fashion. She noted the nail specialist's soft welcome, her efficient way of going about things. *The nail worker provides a pleasant atmosphere*, she thought. Nari, in turn, briefly noted the matron's calm and gracious manners. She uncurled her customer's fingers and went to work without humming.

In the background of Nari's consciousness was her mother's drone, the daughter's memory operating like a watery funnel as opposed to a pond. Her mother would often regale her with the narrative of her origins. The hairdresser had adored telling her daughter about how she had lost track of Nari's father seven months into her pregnancy. He had stopped responding to her calls without warning, running off with the funds she had entrusted him with to start a business for their family. Nari's mother would tell this story with her hands very quickly, smiling very coldly and too widely all the while.

Who was that person who had patted her on the upper back with warm hands? He was a shadowy figure who had briefly shielded her from a storm. Nari had only seen Kai a few times after that one time. The peninsula is small, some say provincial, but vast enough that two individuals may never cross paths again. Nari was not invoking Kai's memory in any focused sense. He was another thread that kept shifting, like the men with whom she relaxed when she was not working. Her regular had become irregular after she lost interest in him. She never collected or maintained people, and she did not try to be held for long in one place either.

After the salarywoman departed, Nari only took a few more customers before closing the shop for the night. She had already contacted a friend about meeting after hours for drinks at a nearby market stall by the ocean for beers, clam stew, and dried anchovies that could be dipped in pepper paste or mayonnaise. Both looked forward to sharing humorous anecdotes and confidences over drinks. Nari's friend was one of the workers who greeted patrons driving into the parking garage of one of the city's most luxurious department stores. She would bow and point to where customers should drive their automobiles, chiming out directions with alacrity. The underground lot's poor air quality caused her to clear her throat often. Lower back problems plagued her as well since she was always standing.

When are you going to go pay your respects to your grandmother now that the weather is getting warmer? her friend inquired.

Nari paused and thought. *I do not know. It is hard to say. My grandmother does not like me anymore.*

Her friend countered, *Is that because you went ahead with getting a goldfish painted on your back, a fish the size of a dragon when you could have ordered something the size of a coin on your inner pelvis?*

That is correct, Nari affirmed. *I had an urge to move through a dark blue expanse with a goldfish's memory, but you are absolutely right. My decision estranged us.*

I will never fully understand you. Her friend leaned back, laughing. *That goldfish is ugly!*

Their exchange reminded Nari that a visit to the capital was overdue. She would take the train back to Seoul to see her grandmother. Her friend was still speaking: *What a drag, a dragon's nest, so brutish and unattractive*—now referring to the hairdresser, not her daughter's goldfish. Nari agreed. What was more, she was intimate enough with this particular friend to permit her these verbal liberties that were forbidden to others, no matter how true they were. A family matter is a family matter. Nari's friend could speak a bit too freely, but she meant well. She was still nice to be around on days when even eating meals felt depleting.

They visited the public baths later that night. They had both refrained from drinking heavily earlier since both had had enough to drink this past week. The bathhouse was crowded and deafening. Male toddlers chortled and shrieked, their little stems flapping as they tottered around. Their grandmothers, mothers, or older sisters trailed after them. Some played alone. Their older brothers, usually four years old and older, conducted themselves with no less glee in the male-only section. While not smelling good, the men's baths did not smell like male urinals, toilets, or locker rooms.

Unconcerned with anyone else, Nari sat in the sauna and stared past the hourglass on the window ledge. If she perspired in the red kiln for the time allotted by the falling sand, the grime on her skin would peel right off under a scrubbing mitt or even her bare hands, rolling into a thin dough along her flesh. The sauna was a wooden bowl that fit eight. It was not reminiscent of an inferno so much as a tepee with a fireplace. Those who entered alongside her could be irksome presences, but Nari would imagine such intruders as rotisserie chickens.

Nari sat in such stillness that her friend may as well have faded away into a bracelet—any bauble—beside her. Older and younger women alike could feel it: they were sitting in the presence of a human goldfish. Nari was an all-seeing eye that was trying to serve as its own lid. To be alive but not excessively sentient—she would maintain this mindset until she had to return to herself for work, where she would strive to be present and overflowing with a winning docility.

Incidentally, Nari had never had her toes sucked or received an entreaty to suck someone else's thus far in her short life. The matter had not come up because she was young, not because of her personal preference. Society forgets that it takes time to become acquainted with one's appetites. Experiences are not that plentiful and spontaneous for the average person. As yet inexperienced in the art of sensualizing the extremities, this raindrop moved through her life at times like a deep-water aquatic. Some goldfish can wander down that far in their dreams, undesirous of anything.

But excessive asceticism can be boring. Nari, like Kai, suspected that Buddha had never returned for a reason. Most people have no interest in spending their lives out of the moment instead of savoring what little moments there are. Too much of Buddhism was dedicated, she felt, to rendering oneself indifferent to the fact that one was dying while the dead remained dead, no matter the Middle Eastern monotheistic religions that pretended that death was a beginning. (Buddhists who emphasize reincarnation do so without the backing of their institutional superiors: the Dalai Lama admits in private that the wheel of life remains a wishful poetic device.) In this context, the goldfish becomes incandescent. Its amnesia is so radical that it forgets to forget about remembering. It does laps, blows kisses to the hermit crab prince next door, and contentedly returns to its castle. It bores itself beyond boredom and begins again. It amuses itself to no end before floating belly-upward to the surface.

There was a slapping noise. It was not Nari's friend gently smacking Nari's shoulder to signal that they should leave the sauna to stave off dehydration. A scrubber was slapping Nari's buttocks and the backs of her upper thighs as she was soaping, exfoliating, oiling, and massaging Nari's entire body. Some save up for electronic devices, others for fashion. Nari gathered what she could for these hour-long bathhouse sessions, where a scrubber-cum-masseuse could breathe some life into her young yet all-too-quickly-coarsening body. She struggled not to shudder too hard when the scrubber oiled her chest, grazing her nipples for a second or two before passing onward, apathetic to her tremors. Everything touched felt nice except her legs and stomach, the latter of which was prone to indigestion from all her late-night drinking and snacking bouts. When the scrubber pressed down on her gut, Nari jerked awake from a painful shooting sensation. Her legs and feet were knotted to the extent that anyone pressing their fingers over them could induce a minor epileptic fit.

But pain was good on the scrubbing table, signifying life rather than rotting. In pain, Nari remained strikingly courteous toward her scrubber. Even as she was particular in what she wanted done, intolerant of any laziness from the one who was responsible for her sauna treatment package, she remained nonabrasive. Her voice did not assume a curt quality. She made herself more diffident, which is no small achievement for one in the service industry (which includes doctors—let us not forget Han). Those in customer service tend to hate everyone eventually, regardless of anyone's temperament, behavior, personal philosophy, friends, or family background. To belong to the service industry is to risk losing any natural desire to be of service to anyone. This loss can be a liberating feeling but not for many and not often.

A drop fell on Nari's face. The scrubber was sweating on her as she was working. The fat around the scrubber's lower abdomen was jiggling as she labored. From one service industry worker to another, Nari thought that her scrubber resembled a hamster. Nari had never been allowed any pets, so this thought was a high compliment.

Voices in the background receded into a pleasant hum as Nari lay on her stomach, a dumpling on a lukewarm plate that was being pinched and poked by a single chopstick. Her friend alerted her that she was going to take a dip in the iciest pool before heading back into the sauna. That friend never paid for any services from the bathhouse staff. She spent her money on nightlife, whether carousing alone or with company. Going out in public was her main source of relief.

To be relieved—overcome all of a sudden by inchoate cravings, Nari distracted herself by making faces at a little girl who was toddling past her table toward the lukewarm pool. The child noticed without smiling back. She remained serious, looking back at Nari once before breaking eye contact, engrossed in the washing bowl she was carrying toward the bath. As humorless as the child was, she did not lack for charm. Nari could feel the masseuse preparing to pour one last round of warm water on her before patting her all over to ensure that she was infused with a springtime vigor.

The train that Nari took back to Seoul to see her grandmother was like a submarine moving deep underwater. It was monsoon season. Little was visible outside the windows as rain pummeled the train so fiercely that the train could not move as quickly as it was wont to. The world outside thundered while the atmosphere within grew more solemn. Every once in a while, the clouds would part and a Homeric dawn could be glimpsed, those rosy, pinkish hues that the Mediterraneans so loved.

As the rain alternated with clear skies, Nari mentally repeated to herself three of her grandmother's favorite stories, which happened to be gathered from a wandering monk. Only one was meant to be a ghost story, but her grandmother could never remember which.

There was the story of a GPS that led its owner to the edge of a cliff. A tipsy salaryman sought to drive himself home from an office party, getting into his car and following the directions given out by his cell phone's navigation system. Something started to bother him, however. The roads seemed funny. He kept driving for a while but could not rid himself of this strange feeling, so he stopped the car, turned off his engine, and tried to get his bearings. It turned out that he had parked his car less than a meter away from a granite abyss constructed by a local firm. As he backed his car away from the precipice in horror, the guiding voice from his phone's mapping application whispered, *Only a little bit farther. Move the car forward. Oh, so close, I almost had him.*

The second story that the monk had told Nari's grandmother had to do with three brothers who all took their lives on the same day. A couple who ran a rural hostel murdered a patron one night with the intent to rob him because they had correctly deduced that he was wealthy. While he was sleeping, they sliced his throat as one would an avocado, leaving him to bleed out. This murdered businessman had left behind three young sons, all four years of age. Within a short span, the hostel keepers somehow gained control over their recent victim's possessions. Ecstatic about their newfound prosperity, the couple set up a string of busy businesses and successfully brought male triplets into the world. Their births were uneventful. By the time these three brothers had reached their early twenties, all were poised to assume promising careers: one in law, the other in politics, and the last in medicine. Yet all three were found dead the day after they had passed their professional exams. All three sons had made a pact to ingest a liquid poison at the same time because they were the reincarnated children of the murdered businessman. In their former lives as the businessman's sons, these three pre-schoolers had been left to fend for themselves without any familiar guardians when their father never came home (their mother had already succumbed to cancer). The triplets decided to go join their father in the afterlife by drowning themselves in a nearby river. Once there, they earned the immortal ferry keeper's permission to return to earth to haunt the couple who had stolen their happiness.

An underground recess was where the monk's last tale ended. A bear and a tiger ventured into a cave for the purpose of metamorphosing into humans. A shaman had told them that if they went into a cave and ate only onions and garlic cloves for one hundred days, they would emerge victorious. In the darkness, the tiger fell into despair, then a deranged boredom, padding out of the cave after a month. The bear stayed in the cave and endured, leaving after the allotted time as an albino woman. The monk had spoken approvingly of the tiger and contemptuously of the bear. Listening until then in rapture, Nari's grandmother had shaken herself alert. *Listen*, she confided to the monk, *my granddaughter is not willful nor comely enough to play either the bear or tiger despite being feral. What is one to do with this whelp in a time and place where mediocrity, unlike in some high-society circles, will not save her?*

Disembarking the train, Nari felt unusual vibrations. Something abnormal was happening. Pigeon cries were resounding throughout the train station. Walking through a glass door to where she could see the rain and wind abating against a red horizon, she heard a strange whistling. The bodies dotting the station's square were all still and staring upward, taut like stalagmites, pikes in a moat. The whistling grew louder. Nari's face was hardening into a rare expression. The goldfish on her back glistened with sweat. Everyone kept looking at their neighbor.

On the day Nari had experienced one of her mother's harshest beatings, she had stored away the memory of a stranger who had reminded her of an elk that had lost its antler. Her mother's friend had folded both of his hands before her face, calling these shapes *herons in flight*. What had that person said? Something regarding birds and bombs, bombs looking like birds, that a hand could be as explosive as a bomb upon the body, but it was easier to think of it as a bird descending to rest on its perch. How funny that today was a day like that person had described years ago, when he had stroked her wet cheeks with shadow birds for hands. It was spring—look, look at those herons falling.

AUTHOR BIO

Ery Shin was born in Ames, Iowa, in 1986. She was raised in Manhattan for the first decade of her life, then Seoul for the second. She received a bachelor's degree in English from Princeton University and a doctorate in the same discipline from the University of Oxford. The author of *Gertrude Stein's Surrealist Years*, a study of Stein's later experimental gestures and their philosophical implications within Hitler's Europe, she is currently an assistant professor of English at the University of Southern Mississippi.